If it be possible, as much as lieth in you,
live peaceably with all men.
–Romans 12:18

Dedicated to all the courageous men and women,
past and present, who run toward danger and
face the worst to keep the rest of us safe and well.

"Stop! It's me!"

"Brad!" Janie faltered for only an instant before recovering. "Run!"

Brad released her and shoved her behind him. "Go!"

Brad grabbed the handle of the door, pinning one arm of her assailant between it and the jamb. The gun was outside in the man's hand, the rest of him still in the building, while he struggled to free himself.

If that thug managed to lift the gun or turn it slightly, he was going to be able to shoot Brad without ever leaving the store!

Oh, no, he isn't. She dropped the plastic bags on the ground and reached into the closest one. Finger on the spray nozzle of the foaming cleanser, she dashed back to Brad just as he lost his hold on the door and was thrown out of the way.

Janie attacked. The foam hit its target.

The thug screamed, dropped his weapon and covered his stinging eyes with both hands.

"You got him. And I have his gun," Brad shouted. "Let's go!"

Valerie Hansen was thirty when she awoke to the presence of the Lord in her life and turned to Jesus. She now lives in a renovated farmhouse on the breathtakingly beautiful Ozark Plateau of Arkansas and is privileged to share her personal faith by telling the stories of her heart for Love Inspired. Life doesn't get much better than that!

Books by Valerie Hansen

Love Inspired Suspense

Emergency Responders

Fatal Threat
Marked for Revenge
On the Run

True Blue K-9 Unit: Brooklyn

Tracking a Kidnapper

True Blue K-9 Unit

Trail of Danger

Military K-9 Unit

Bound by Duty
Military K-9 Unit Christmas
"Christmas Escape"

Classified K-9 Unit

Special Agent

Visit the Author Profile page at Harlequin.com for more titles.

ON THE RUN

VALERIE HANSEN

LOVE INSPIRED SUSPENSE
INSPIRATIONAL ROMANCE

LOVE INSPIRED® SUSPENSE
INSPIRATIONAL ROMANCE

ISBN-13: 978-1-335-58103-7

On the Run

Copyright © 2021 by Valerie Whisenand

This edition published by arrangement with Harlequin Books S.A.

For questions and comments about the quality of this book, please contact us
at CustomerService@Harlequin.com.

Love Inspired
22 Adelaide St. West, 40th Floor
Toronto, Ontario M5H 4E3, Canada
www.Harlequin.com

Printed in U.S.A.

ONE

"*Code Silver.* All personnel, be advised, we have a *Code Silver.*"

The male voice blaring over the PA system sounded a lot calmer than Janie Kirkpatrick felt. In the three years she'd been an emergency room nurse she'd never encountered a code silver except as a drill. Now, she was staring down the barrel of a real handgun, the object of the hospital's cryptic warning. It didn't matter that this firearm wasn't actually silver, the threat was frighteningly clear.

Senses heightened beyond belief, Janie masked her fear and faced the three rough-looking men who had delivered a wounded comrade to the ER and laid him out on a gurney. "You can put the gun away," she said. "We'll care for your friend the same way we would any patient."

When the oldest of the four gestured with the pistol in his meaty hand, she suppressed a shudder.

"Then get to it," he said. "Tim's bleedin' out."

Where was a doctor? Where were the other nurses? Janie wished she could see through the privacy curtains that had been pulled around that small treatment area to close it off.

The tallest of the four men shouldered forward and cautiously placed his hand across the top of the pistol. "Hey, if you scare her too bad she won't be worth a hoot, Boss." His voice was deep with just a hint of gruffness.

The leader jerked the gun away, then aimed it directly at Janie. She could tell he was near the end of what little patience he'd had to begin with. Her knees weakened. She began to perspire despite the air-conditioning. "Please..."

The tall man stepped closer to her and spoke quietly. "You'll be fine. I suggest you let me cut Tim's clothes away from his wound while you check his vitals. Blood pressure's probably low. He was shot a couple of hours ago and I haven't been able to stop the bleeding. That's why we brought him here."

Eyes wide, Janie stared at the stranger towering over her five-foot-three-inch height. Strong, dark-haired and a healthy thirtysomething, he looked more like a renegade than a medic thanks to long hair, a scruffy, unshaven chin and worn denim clothing, yet he seemed to have useful knowledge.

As her blue eyes momentarily connected with his somber gaze she searched in vain for a flicker of anything that would tell her whether or not she might have found an ally.

Using her stethoscope she listened to the moaning patient's heartbeat and breathing, then spoke to her possible helper. "I'm getting a fast pulse. Lung sounds are not good. BP is low. He may be bleeding into the pleural cavity, too."

"Yeah, that's what I was afraid of," the man murmured as he cut away the last of the patient's shirt and dropped the pieces on the floor. "You want to start an IV?"

"I was about to."

The armed man interrupted, "Get a move on."

Janie had been proceeding cautiously. Now that she had at least one aide who seemed halfway normal, she regained more of her usual professional air. Hands fisted on her hips, shoulders back, she said, "Look, mister. This will all go a lot faster if you stop pointing that stupid gun at me."

"Then quit stalling," the man ordered. "I know what you're doin'. You're waitin' for the cops to get here. Well, I'm not fallin' for it." He motioned to the man who had been assisting her. "Let's go, Brad. You're done playin' doctor."

"I'll stay a little longer. You guys go."

"Nothin' doin'. Either you're one of us or you're not."

The man's—Brad's—eyes locked on Janie's. She could tell he was trying to communicate something but had no idea what it might be. Did he expect her to read his mind?

"You can go," she said, feigning calmness. "I can start the IV by myself."

"What if he arrests?"

"Then I'll call a code blue and somebody will show up with a crash cart."

"Will they?" Brad's glance darted to the speaker in the ceiling.

So, she thought, *he knows what our code means*. That might or might not be a good sign. Where was hospital security? Why didn't she hear any sirens? Had so little time actually elapsed that it was too soon to expect backup?

Despite the strongest willpower she possessed, she couldn't stop trembling. A needle needed to go into this patient's vein but her hand was shaking too much to insert it properly. The thugs didn't seem to notice, but Brad did.

His warm, firm grip on her wrist convinced her to pass the catheter needle to him. Relinquishing control was an unacceptable action for a licensed, trained nurse, but at that moment she saw no other alternative. If the patient's blood pressure dropped much lower it would be next to impossible to find a viable vein. If she couldn't find one, somebody had to.

"Hey, lady, what do you think you're doin'?" the elder thug shouted. "Get back to work!"

"I am. I—"

He was on her in a heartbeat, and because Brad was concentrating on starting the IV, there was no one standing ready to defend her.

A meaty hand closed on her arm. Pain shot up to her shoulder as Janie was jerked off her feet and thrown across the cubicle. Her upper back hit a metal supply cart and sent it rolling and rattling through the open space at the bottom of the privacy curtains. She'd had patients abuse her before but they had been delusional due to medication or disease. This man, these men, were just like her older brothers had been. Cruel to the bone. Well, they weren't going to best her.

Pushing off the floor with both hands, Janie stumbled to her feet. Everything hurt. Her head was spinning. By the time she was fully erect, however, anger had dulled the pain. Nobody was going to treat her that way anymore. Nobody.

Painful memories rushed to surface. Memories of abuse and tears and wondering if she was worthy of any life at all. As soon as she'd been old enough to manage alone, she'd fled her mean-spirited siblings and had learned self-defense, putting herself through nursing school by teaching other women how to physically fight back. Now, it was high time to employ those skills herself.

She didn't strike a karate pose or shout, she simply braced herself and waited for one or more of the men to come after her. The gunman gestured for his youngest cohort to attack. Janie watched his eyes narrow before he began to smile and start toward her.

Meeting the wiry man's lunge with a sidestep she reached out, grabbed his closest arm, ducked under it and flipped him onto his back without difficulty. He hit the floor with a thud, then lay there, stunned, while Janie stepped out of his reach and readied for another assault. Her eyes swept the cubicle, assessing her adversaries. The prostrate thug would soon recover and get up, she knew, but her immediate concern was the armed older man. The one they'd called Boss.

Roaring, he brought the gun to bear on her body and took dead aim at her heart.

Janie froze, too far from the armed man to use her skills, and positive any such moves would cause him to shoot.

Brad charged into the fray from behind, striking the boss's outstretched arm and sending the gun sliding across the floor.

That changed everything. Janie whirled. Assessed. Decided. The wiry one she'd flipped was regaining his wits and crawling toward the weapon. There was no time to run closer and kick it away so she dived in that direction, landing atop her prostrate enemy.

His longer arms reached the cold metal first. Janie clasped his wrist with both hands. He flipped her onto her back, yet she held fast. They rolled together, grappling for the gun. Janie's arms were shorter but strong. If she failed to gain control she knew she was in deep trouble.

Training made her continue to hold his wrist with all her strength. She got her knees under her first, shouted hoarsely, then threw her whole weight behind the effort to bend it back. As long as she kept holding him at an angle that kept the gun's muzzle pointing away from her she'd be okay.

He screamed in agony but didn't let go. Neither did she.

Less than ten feet away, the boss was being restrained by her unexpected cohort, Brad, so no help was coming to quickly aid the thug with his finger on the trigger.

Frantic to hold on, Janie leaned into the defensive grip. Heard the pop of dislocating joints as ligaments and tendons in his wrist let go. Empathetically sharing his pain, her stomach clenched.

The man shrieked.

Janie was thrown off balance. She fell against him, the gun pressed between their bodies. He outweighed her by at least fifty pounds, which gave him a leverage advantage.

His acrid breath was hot on her face. She closed her eyes and reacted instinctively, slamming her forehead into his nose.

The gun jerked, firing. There was a deafening bang!

In the midst of the melee, while the nurse had been fighting back, Brad had realized why she'd seemed familiar. It had been years since he and other patrol officers had responded to domestic violence calls at a house outside Kansas City, but he was pretty sure this was the same young woman, even though the last name on her hospital ID didn't match his memory. As a teen, she'd been the helpless victim of a destructive family. It was good to see she'd escaped the constant abuse and had grown up to become a useful member of society. But how could he continue to help her without blowing his cover?

He'd been assigned to infiltrate this criminal organization and he needed to continue to prove his allegiance to Speevey. Besides, the sooner he hustled the older man out of there, the better it would be for all concerned, especially the nurse.

Grabbing his "boss" by the shoulders, he spun him around and pushed him toward the door. "Go. I'll take care of this."

Speevey put on the brakes. "No way. We're not leavin' without my Bubba."

"Let him stay here with Tim."

"And wind up in jail? Not hardly. We'll come back for Timmy as soon as he's been doctored up."

Because he was grasping the man's shoulders, Brad felt the moment when reality slipped through. The wild gunshot had caused everyone to duck, yes, but one of them was down because he was gravely injured.

"Bub!" Speevey roared like an animal as he dived for his prostrate son, kicking Janie aside as though she were weightless. He gathered the thin young man in his arms, mindless of the crimson stain spreading from an abdominal wound.

Edging sideways, Brad tried to slip between the tragic tableau on the ER floor and the nurse. He could tell she was attempting to gather her wits. No telling what her reaction would be once she realized that the bullet had injured someone. Even cops were traumatized when they had to use lethal force, and this tenderhearted civilian was liable to take it even harder.

Plus, time was running out, Brad reasoned. He didn't dare carry law enforcement identification for fear of being accidentally outed, so the cops in this part of Missouri had no idea who he really was. If he was forced to tell them, all his previous time undercover would probably be for nothing. Speevey wasn't the top man he'd been assigned to find but there were enough personal connections to give him hope of solving a series of gang killings, one of which had cost his old friend and police chief, Wes Winterhaven, his only son.

Until Tim had been shot by a rival gang that morning, all Brad had needed to do was wait until he'd gathered enough solid proof to call in the FBI. Now, everything had changed. And not for the better.

He pulled Speevey up and dragged him toward the exit. The man lying on the gurney was moaning but there was no sound from the one on the floor.

"Pressure bandage," Brad said gruffly, directing his instructions to Janie. "Better hurry."

Her semilucid stare slid from him and Speevey to the man collapsed on the floor. Her expression changed as she realized what he was saying and made sense of the mayhem in front of her.

"You can handle this," Brad told her. "Now move."

Instead of waiting to see if she complied, Brad trusted the hospital situation to God—and a capable staff—and hustled Speevey outside.

A late-summer hot spell lingered ahead of a predicted cold front, creating the ideal trigger for thunderstorms. Wind ripped dried leaves from half-bare oaks and sycamores lining the street. Blowing dust smelled musty. Thunder rumbled.

"Into my truck," Brad ordered.

Weeping, Speevey didn't argue. That was just as well since Brad was fairly certain that Bubba's injury was going to be fatal regardless of the treatment he was about to receive. He'd seen guys gut-shot while in combat overseas. It wasn't pretty.

He pushed the old man into the front seat of his pickup and drove slowly out of the lot by a rear entrance. Approaching patrol cars going the opposite direction ignored him, partly due to his turtle-like pace. He'd counted on that happening.

Now, all he had to do was stick close to Speevey and hope he'd reach out to higher-ups for a replacement crew. There were drugs to deliver, quotas to make, money to collect. Without either of his sons, the old man would need outside help. And Detective Bradley Benton, aka criminal Brad Ross, was going to make sure he was right in the middle of it.

Janie was weary but not happy when she was relieved of duty. "I can still work. Please, let me stick this one out."

"No way," the charge nurse told her. "I have someone coming in to replace you in the schedule. Go home."

Janie's eyes misted. "It wasn't my fault. He was trying to shoot me."

"I know that and the police know that, Kirkpatrick. Nobody's blaming you. But you look like you just ran a marathon through a jungle and had to fight for every step. So clock out. Go take a nice hot shower and kick back. Hug your little dog if it'll help you unwind. I'll rework the schedule to give you a week off. If you need more, let me know. You have plenty of sick time built up."

"It's not about the money," Janie insisted. "Those men. So young. So sad."

"And so stupid," her superior added. "It's not anybody's fault but theirs that one is gone and the other is clinging to life. If you want to blame somebody, blame their father. He brought them in to us, right?"

"Right." Janie hadn't held back information about her erstwhile helper but she hadn't volunteered a lot of detail, either. It didn't take a genius to see that his background was different than that of the others. So was his speech. When he talked about medical matters he sounded professional, although he'd never claimed to be.

Regardless, she reasoned, Brad was special. Anybody who stood up and defended her the way he had deserved the benefit of the doubt and she was certainly ready to give it to him. Truth to tell, she might also be ready to like him, regardless.

TWO

Speevey was ranting and raving as he paced the deserted reaches of the motel parking lot, his cell phone pressed to his ear. "No. I've gotta go get my boys first."

Listening, Brad wondered how long the old man intended to argue with whoever was on the line. Even the toughest criminal had to bow to whoever ran the show, and it sounded as if Speevey was going too far with his refusals.

"All right, all right. I've got one man left standin' who can make the pickup. Where and when?... Okay. Got it."

Speevey scribbled on a scrap of paper and thrust it at Brad as he ended his call. "Be at that corner for the pickup at noon and bring the goods back here. If I'm gone, wait for me."

"How long? How far away are you going to be?"

The lined face hardened. "Not far. I'm goin' back for my boys and my car—and to take care of unfinished business. I've got a score to settle with a certain nurse."

Although Brad was certain only Tim was still alive, he pretended otherwise. He reached for his leather bomber jacket and eyed the gray sky. "You'll need me and my pickup to help move them, especially if it rains. Let me come with you."

"You just do your job and stay out of my personal space. You kept beggin' to be trusted. Well, now's your chance."

"Yes, sir, Mr. Speevey. I'm on it."

Brad wheeled and started to circle his truck. A loud, harsh "Hey!" sounded behind him.

He froze, his hand gripping the door handle. "What?"

"This," Speevey said, reaching into his pants pocket.

For a split second, Brad thought he was going for another gun. When a small, black cell phone sailed through the air toward him instead, he caught it instinctively. Getting the phone was a sign he was earning more trust.

Without another word he climbed behind the wheel, tossing the cell phone onto the seat. He didn't dare show up at the hospital himself but now he could easily call his chief and ask him to arrange for a protection detail. Things were looking up.

Brad whipped into a parking lot three blocks from the motel, left his truck idling and grabbed up the phone. His call went to Chief Winterhaven's private voice mail. Leaving a detailed message was out of the question since they didn't know who to trust. So what were his other options? He saw only one and took it.

"Springfield Medical. How may I direct your call?"

"Nurse Janie Kirkpatrick in the ER, please."

"Sorry. She's clocked out."

"Okay, listen, this is Officer… Tucker," Brad said, hoping his memory for names and precincts was as sharp as ever and praying he'd picked a feasible name out of those he'd memorized. "I misplaced her phone number after that incident today in your ER. It's vital that I reach her ASAP. Can you help me?"

"I'm sorry, Officer. We don't give out employees' private information. Why don't you contact the cops who were on scene? Maybe they can help you."

He was about to start pleading when she added, "Hold on. Here's one of them." Brad heard her speaking in the background. "It's some cop. Says his name is Tucker. He's asking for Kirkpatrick's phone number and I'm not allowed to give it out."

A genial male voice came on the line. "Hey, Tuck, up to your old tricks? If you wanted her number you should have just asked her for it."

Brad couldn't believe he'd gotten this far with such a flimsy ruse. "Yeah, yeah." He was working to keep his breathing even and his voice muted. "Give a guy a break."

"Okay. Hold on. But you'll owe me one." Reciting an area code and phone number, the cop chuckled. "Have fun."

All Brad said was, "Thanks," before ending that call and punching in Janie's number.

He'd almost given up when a sweet voice said, "Hello?"

"Ms. Kirkpatrick? Janie Kirkpatrick?"

"Yes. Who is this?"

"A friend. You're in danger. Don't ask questions, just hit the road. Now. And don't tell anybody where you're going."

"Why should I believe you? Who are you?"

"The guy from the ER."

He heard her loud intake of breath. "Brad?"

"Yeah. My boss is coming after you. You need to run. It's not safe for you to stay anywhere in Springfield. Keep this number in case you need help and let me know you're safe once you get far enough away."

He thought he heard her snort derisively right before she drawled, "Oh, *right*." A little dog was yapping in the background, as if she had taken the phone away from her ear and was about to hang up.

"Wait!" Brad was desperate. "You have to believe me."

"Why should I?"

That was an excellent question considering how little she knew about him and the trauma of the events in the ER. "I can't give you any details," he said soberly.

"Then goodbye."

"No! Think. You met me. Did I seem like the others? Really?"

There was a brief hesitation before she said, "No," but Brad wasn't satisfied that she was taking him seriously enough so he resorted to pleading. "Please, give me the benefit of the doubt. You know I didn't belong with those other men. You could sense it. I'm sure you could."

"You're assuming a lot," Janie replied.

"Because a lot is hanging on this conversation," Brad said.

"Like what?"

He blew a noisy sigh before he spoke. "Like your survival."

Janie knew she could be the victim of a hoax, yet there was something genuine about that man. Plus, it wasn't smart to ignore such a specific warning. Not without investigating it. But how?

Staring at her phone, she decided to save the number Brad had called from, just in case. Even if she didn't need it herself she could always turn it over to the police. That's what a normal person would do.

"But I'm not normal, am I, Pixie?" she murmured to her dog. Pixie whirled in circles at her feet, yipping happily at being noticed.

"Yes, baby. I know you love me, anyway. I just wish…"

Scooping up the little wiggly dog, she held her close to draw comfort as regret washed over her. It didn't matter that the wiry thug had been trying to shoot her. He was the one who had been killed and for that she was truly sorry. Deep down, however, she was also glad to have been the one who had survived and that bothered her enough to pray, "Father, forgive me."

Long ago she had vowed to break the cycle of abuse she'd been trapped in for so long. That was why she'd chosen to change her last name, become a nurse and help people. It was also why she felt ashamed about being the survivor of the hand-to-hand battle. Had she somehow reinforced her strength via anger or a wish for retribution? Was it possible that the darkness lurking in all three of her brothers had stained her heart a little, too? After all, they'd had the same parents.

"I'm not like them," Janie insisted.

Pixie obviously agreed because she slurped Janie's cheek.

Although she said, "Enough!" the messy show of affection helped draw her back to the present problem. She looked around her small apartment, realizing she had no way to keep out a determined assassin and no means of defense other than her martial arts skill. Plus, she had Pixie to worry about.

If she was anything, Janie concluded, she was smart. And wary. Why not go straight to the local police instead of going on the run? Because she needed more details about her supposed enemies before showing up at a police station insisting she was the target of assassins. A lot more details if she hoped to be believed.

Her mind countered with the unsettling premise that the call had been a ruse and somebody was waiting to pick her off as soon as she stepped outside.

Was she taking a bigger risk by delaying her departure until dark? Would Brad know the answer?

Maybe, she reasoned, but no way was she going to call back and ask him. Saving her life once—or more—didn't automatically make him an honest man. Considering the crowd he ran with, there wasn't anything on earth that would convince her to trust him *that* much.

A quick detour past the hospital hadn't taken Brad far from the rendezvous point on Battlefield Boulevard. To his relief, there were patrol cars stationed outside the ER as well as around front. That would do for now.

Since he'd heard high-pitched barking in the background of his call to Janie he'd been assured she was at home. That would give her extra time to escape—if she actually did as he'd instructed. Considering her disbelieving attitude he figured it was a toss-up.

In the meantime, he'd fulfilled his assigned task and had gone back to the motel with the duffel of drugs. Speevey was there waiting for him. So were two other men whose countenance made the former Speevey trio look like upstanding citizens. One of these men seemed tense while the second, a balding, smarmy guy, stared daggers at everybody. Empty bottles and cans indicated that they had been drinking.

Brad swaggered in. "Started the party without me?"

"There's cops all over the hospital," Speevey said, slurring his words. "Couldn't get back in." He smiled and gestured with his whole arm. "Called in reinforcements."

"I see that." Brad stuck out his hand. Nobody shook it so he backed off. "What's the plan?"

"People are workin' on it. Soon as we find out where that nurse lives, we'll head over there."

"I can scout it out for you. Let you know what she's up to," Brad offered.

Speevey had tears in his eyes when he said, "I'll tell you what she'll be doin'. She'll be dyin' just like my Bubba did if I have any say in it."

A hidden shiver shot up Brad's spine and prickled the hair at the nape of his neck. What he needed to do was somehow ally himself with the new men and be taken back to the main organization instead of being eliminated as excess baggage. He was trying to work out how to accomplish that when the bald thug took a call.

Listening intently, Brad didn't hear him say a thing except, "Got it," before hanging up. When the others started for the door, Brad followed. Speevey paid no attention to him but Baldy did. "You. Stay right here and guard the product. We'll take care of business and be back for you when we're done."

"Sure thing." His gaze took in all three expressions. Only Speevey seemed enthused about their mission. The others deadpanned, making them hard to read and convincing Brad they were trouble with a capital *T*.

The door slammed behind them. Brad slipped his hand into his jacket pocket to reassure himself that his cell phone was still there. He'd half expected the others to confiscate it but he supposed doing so would have been too transparent, particularly if they intended to return and execute him as an unwanted witness once they were through with Speevey.

At this point he figured he had two choices. He could sit there like a duck in a shooting gallery and wait for them to decide to eliminate him. Or he could take off and see if he could locate the nurse before they did. His only advantage, as far as he knew, was having her phone number.

He whipped out his phone and redialed, surprised when she answered. Sounds of traffic in the background melded with car radio music and the swish of windshield wipers.

"Sounds like you're on the road. That's good," Brad said. When he got no reply, he continued, "Listen. If I have your phone number, others will soon have it, too. I'm serious about this, Ms. Kirkpatrick. You need to take steps to cover your tracks."

Pausing, he was about to resume giving her instructions when she spoke. "You really were telling the truth." It wasn't a question.

"Yes. As I said, I can't explain everything but you can trust me. Do you have plenty of cash on you?"

"Some. I stopped at a couple of ATMs and withdrew my limit."

"Good. I'd tell you to dump your phone and buy a new one except I may need to get in touch with you again." Picturing her flipping Bubba over her head, he almost smiled. "I'm afraid you might try to ditch me, too, if you bought a new phone."

"It did occur to me."

"Smart lady. The thing is, you need me on your side."

"Why is that?"

"Because I want to help you." Brad waited for an argument. When he didn't get one he realized she had disconnected.

He redialed.

Janie said, "Leave me alone," instead of hello.

"Wait! Don't hang up again."

"Why shouldn't I?"

"Because—because you know me."

"What?" The music faded as if she'd turned down the radio.

"You know me. Think back. Kansas City. Seven or eight years ago."

"Were you a friend of my brothers'?"

"No! No," Brad said quickly. "The opposite."

"Keep talking."

Brad was trapped by his own partial confession. If he didn't explain, she was going to hang up again. If he did tell her who he really was and she was overtaken, she might inadvertently reveal too much. However, since he figured he was inches from being on a hit list, anyway, taking Janie into his confidence was the smartest move.

"I'm a police officer, Ms. Kirkpatrick. I was working undercover when Tim, one of the men I was with, was shot. When we brought him to the hospital, I thought I recognized you from an old case back in KC."

"What kind of case?"

There was enough doubt in her voice to

let him know he was on the right track. "Domestic abuse," he said solemnly. "If you're the person I think you are, you had a couple of really rough brothers."

"Three. There were three."

"But your name wasn't Kirkpatrick, was it?"

"No. I changed it when I left home. My mother had passed away and my dad spent every cent he had on alcohol. I just wanted to disappear."

"I can understand that."

Waiting for her reply, Brad pictured the person she had once been and contrasted that image with her current persona. The woman had literally transformed herself from a scared teen to a capable nurse who wasn't afraid to do what she knew was right, and he had to admire her.

Finally, he broke the silence. "Are you still there?"

"Yes, I…"

Tension in her tone was unsettling. "Talk to me. What's going on?"

"There's a big black car behind me. It keeps changing lanes when I do."

"Do you think you're being followed? Is it Speevey?"

"Can't tell. The windows are tinted really dark."

"Okay, try to lose them."

"Hah!" Cynicism tinged Janie's reply. "What do you think I've been doing?"

"Where are you? Tell me where you are!"

Instead, he heard the screeching of tires, the yipping of her little dog and a gasp from Janie.

"Talk to me! Where?" Brad shouted into the phone.

"Campbell and… Seminole!" She broke off, letting out a bloodcurdling scream.

"Janie!"

THREE

Rain was stopping but had left the road-
way wet. Janie had shrieked when she'd
fumbled her phone and almost lost control of her compact car as she'd skidded
around the corner onto Seminole. Traffic was congested. That was a plus and a
minus. It helped, up to a point. As long
as she didn't let herself get bogged down
she might be okay.

No one had taught her defensive driving
but some moves came naturally, thanks
to surging adrenaline. Having a small car
was also to her advantage because she
could slip in and out of the lines of cars
more easily than the larger vehicle she was
certain was following her.

A distant voice was yelling at her. *The phone!* What had happened to her phone?

Pixie had wiggled out the top of her pink canvas carrier and was digging at the space between the passenger seat and center console. "Is my cell down there, baby?" Janie asked, not bothered by the idea she was asking a dog. "Can you get it? Get it, Pixie!"

The little dog jumped to the floor and began scratching at the narrow space, her little white paws flying. She was growling and barking while the slim cell phone kept making noises Janie couldn't decipher.

She checked her rearview mirrors. The black car wasn't there anymore. Had it missed the turn? She certainly hoped it had, although that wasn't enough to convince her she was in the clear.

Pixie was still yipping and trying to dig the cell phone loose. Janie made a cautious turn onto Jefferson, watching both directions in case her enemies were circling the block. The idea that they might be doing so convinced her to make another quick turn onto Crestview and pull into the small parking lot at a neighborhood park. There, she hid herself among a line of cars, turned off the engine and ducked down, picking up the dropped phone once it was within reach.

She and Brad were still connected and he was shouting, "North or south on Seminole? Janie! Answer me!"

"Hush," she managed as soon as he paused to take a breath. "I'm fine for now."

"You scared me to death, lady. Where are you? What's been happening?"

"I dropped the phone when I turned a sharp corner and Pixie's been trying to dig it out ever since."

"I heard her."

"Yeah, sorry about that." She raised on one elbow to scan the street and surroundings. "I think I got away. I'm just not sure how long it'll be before they find me."

"Are you parked or driving?"

"Parked. I couldn't reach the phone without stopping."

"You need to lose yourself in a big parking lot, like maybe that one at the Springfield Sportsman's Complex."

"Too far away," she said in a near whisper.

"All right. I'll come get you."

"No way. I can disappear without your help. I did it before and I can do it again."

"At what cost?" Brad asked.

"What do you mean?"

"The people you work with at the hospital, for starters. We need to be sure that they're protected. And then there's your career. How do you expect to get a job as a nurse if you have to change your name again and can't take your credentials with you?"

"You're a big beautiful ray of sunshine, aren't you?" she tossed back sarcastically.

"Just being practical. I have police connections and I can have your friends protected, to start with. I can also use your help identifying the head of the criminal organization."

"*My* help? That's ridiculous."

"Hear me out. I was supposed to be working my way into the confidence of Speevey and his bosses but he went off the rails when his sons were hurt."

"So? What does that have to do with me?"

"Simple. Revenge. And since I was working with Speevey, chances are the organization plans to eliminate all of us, him included, to tie up loose ends."

Her sarcasm was back. "Peachy."

"I'm telling it like it is."

"According to you. Look, Brad, or whatever your real name is, I don't trust you any farther than I can throw you—and maybe not even that far. Stop trying to find me. I can handle myself without your interference. Understand?"

"I understand, but clearly you don't," he shot back. "Battlefield Park? Is that where you are?"

Janie stuffed her little dog into the canvas carrier, started her car and put it in gear. "Give it up. I'm not telling you. Period."

She was about to break the connection

when he shouted, "Holland and Glen-wood! There's a little park near where you turned. I'll be right there. Look for my white pickup truck."

Janie revved the engine, whipped the wheel and fishtailed out the driveway onto the narrow, residential street. She was not going to be anywhere near there when he arrived. And she was certainly not going to put her trust, her life, in the hands of a man who kept company with drug ped-dlers and murderers, no matter how at-tractive or appealing she'd found him to be.

"What if I'm making a big mistake?" she asked herself. "What if he turns out to be an honest man, somebody I should have trusted?"

The little white dog in the carrier beside her had been quiet until they recrossed Jefferson. Then Pixie stuck her head out the top flap again and began to bark, mak-ing the fine hairs at the back of Janie's neck prickle.

"I should never have listened to that so-called cop and let him scare me more," Janie told the dog. "Or you, either. Hush. No barking."

She may as well have been telling the wind to stop blowing. Pixie had more to say and was intent on expressing herself. She'd been noisy ever since she was a puppy and didn't seem to be outgrowing the tendency.

Janie finally resorted to using her sternest voice while pulling to the curb to solve the problem. "No. No barking."

She gave the soft fur at the top of the dog's head a gentle push, tucked its ears down and leaned sideways to zip the opening on the top of the carrier. When Pixie couldn't see out, she was less prone to getting excited and making excessive noise.

"I'm sorry, baby, but you gave me no choice. I need to pay attention to my driving, not to you."

As she began to straighten, Janie peered out over the dashboard. She was merely checking traffic, not expecting to spot

Brad's white truck or anybody else she recognized.

Her eyes widened. She ducked back down. A big, black SUV was cruising past slowly rather than driving the same speed as the rest of the traffic. It had passed her without stopping. Would it be back? Or was she feeling panicky for nothing?

Another quick peek showed the SUV slowly turning the corner. The passenger's wet side window was rolling down now that the rain had ended. A man's bare elbow rested on the opening. She saw his head turn. Pause. Turn away, then snap back while he pointed. At her.

It was her enemies. It had to be. They were committed to completing the turn because of surrounding traffic but one of them had spotted her. She knew they had. If she hadn't had to pull over to take care of Pixie they could have driven right up behind her!

Adrenaline surged. Janie whipped the car into a tight U-turn and sped back the way she had come. Crossed one side street. Approached a second.

A white pickup truck was pulling up to a stop sign on her right, preparing to enter the intersection. If that was Brad he probably didn't know what she was driving and might not recognize her. Did she want him to? Was it time to swallow the bitter pill and admit she could use some help? Only one city block and some traffic separated her from the suspicious SUV.

Janie hit her brakes, honked her horn in three short bursts, three long, then three short again. *SOS.* Did he get the message?

It seemed to take forever for the white truck to turn to follow her but turn it did.

Janie almost cheered.

Three more unexpected turns to form a zigzagging course and she was positive the white truck was on her *trail*. All that was left to do was pray that the driver was on her *side*.

Brad couldn't decide whether to be angry or glad. He finally settled on mixed emotions. That driver had to be Janie. Who else would honk a melody at him for no reason. His brain abruptly jumped to the conclusion she'd been trying to send Morse code. That might not be logical for most civilians but it fit her quirky personality.

He glanced in his mirrors and noted a black vehicle gaining on them, which meant that the third in line was truly speeding. Janie had been keeping her speed right at the top of what was legal and safe. He'd matched it as soon as he'd caught up. Therefore, the third member of their convoy was really pushing the limits, particularly in a residential neighborhood.

Trying to get her to answer her phone again, Brad kept calling. He saw her glance down to her right every time it rang but she didn't pick it up. Finally, he saw a chance to pull parallel to her and shout across.

Janie met his challenge and rolled down her window. "What?"

"Change your mind?" he hollered.

Instead of replying she looked into her rearview mirror. Brad did the same. A dusty black vehicle with a heavy welded bumper and grille guard was still coming.

He saw her eyes widen. She looked back at him. "If that's who I think it is, yes."

"Smart lady. Pull ahead. I'll stall them."

She was gone before he'd finished speaking, leaving a cloud of gray exhaust in her wake. Brad knew enough about cars to worry. Janie's compact was old and undoubtedly mechanically unsound. If she was like most drivers he knew, male or female, she hadn't checked the oil or water levels in ages. Run low on either and she was liable to blow up her engine, particularly driving the way she currently was.

Brad slowed, concentrating on the massive bumper behind him. A factory-ready SUV was formidable in its own right. Add the kind of after-market equipment that this one sported and it became a two-ton battering ram. A little car like Janie's would be easy to push off the road or cause to crash.

His hands tightened on his steering wheel. Even his full-size pickup truck was no match for this pursuer.

Slowing and keeping to the center of the two-lane road as much as possible, Brad watched the behemoth inching closer. Then it stopped. Just stopped and sat there. Why? What was the driver planning?

Up ahead, Brad saw Janie turn left. If she was smart she'd hop onto Highway 65 or 44 and beat it out of town. In the meantime he could hopefully slow her pursuers enough to let her escape.

The few seconds he'd used to check on Janie were not advantageous. When he glanced back into his rearview mirror, he saw the SUV growing larger and larger. It was coming for him, hard and fast!

Brad jammed the accelerator to the floorboard. His truck engine roared. Rear tires squealed and laid tracks of rubber. Moments later he was hit so hard from behind he lost control.

The right side of his pickup climbed the

curb, took out a mailbox, sideswiped a tree and came to rest against a parked delivery van. Sounds of the collision echoed up and down the otherwise quiet street. People popped out of their houses, aghast, phones in hand. Most took photos, waiting for something else to happen. A few, Brad hoped, were calling 911.

The SUV that had hit him had deployed airbags for its driver and front seat passenger and they were still struggling to push them away. His truck was so old it wasn't equipped with that kind of crash protection, so he didn't have to fight inflated white bags. He did, however, wonder if it would still run. The engine might be okay but it was pretty hard to steer with a crumpled fender, not to mention the possibility that the collision had damaged his radiator.

Brad climbed out stiffly, leaning on the left side of his truck, and worked his way to the hood to see for himself. The damage was worse than he'd imagined. A tire was off the rim and that whole wheel was skewed. His head spun. His breathing was ragged. His ribs ached from where the seat belt had grabbed to keep him from sailing through the windshield.

But Janie escaped, he reminded himself.

Pride was short-lived. Two burly guys were climbing out of the black SUV, which had sustained little damage thanks to its heavy grille cover. The driver drew a gun. The passenger was talking into a cell phone. He, too, was armed.

Brad instinctively reached for the duty holster that wasn't there. His jaw muscles clenched. This was not looking good.

Janie heard the crash. So did Pixie. The little dog sounded as if she was trying to tear her travel box apart at the seams.

Slowing, Janie watched for Brad's truck. The idea that he'd been involved in the terrible accident she'd just heard happening wouldn't go away, no matter how hard she tried to convince herself he was fine. Somehow, she knew he wasn't fine. Not fine at all. And it was her fault because he'd been trying to protect her.

Turn around, her conscience ordered. *Go back. Help him.*

"No, no, no," Janie insisted. She coasted to the edge of the road, leaving the car idling while she considered her next move. Emergency medicine was sometimes the only thing that stood between survival and death. But what about *her* survival? Brad had insisted that she was in danger from criminals and the actions of the SUV driver had reinforced that warning.

Suppose Brad had neutralized them via the crash? she asked herself. Or suppose he was badly hurt and needed medical aid ASAP? Her breath caught as her mind considered other scenarios. Bystanders could also need her help.

All the times in the past when she had wept and prayed for someone, anyone, to save her from her brothers' abuse flooded her memory. How could she not go back and render aid?

Janie closed her eyes for a momentary

prayer followed by a plan of sorts. She'd circle the block where she'd left Brad and come in from the opposite side. Then she'd take stock of the situation at a distance and make her final decision whether or not to proceed. That was logical.

"And not quite as foolish as facing danger head-on."

She checked the zippers on the dog carrier, then got out and moved it to the floor behind her for added safety before fastening her seat belt again and pulling back into traffic. A knot of cars was crowding the intersection behind her. Could they see the accident from there? Probably, meaning her original plan was feasible.

Hands fisted on the steering wheel, senses on high alert, Janie turned one corner, then the next. From the final side street she could see everything, and the sight made her heart twist, her breathing becoming shallow and rapid.

Brad was standing near his wrecked truck, backing away from two evidently armed men, his hands in the air, a duffel bag slung over his shoulders.

"Facing danger head-on is right, after all," she murmured as every muscle in her body tensed, ready for fight or flight.

She knew she could bypass this final turn and probably get away while the thugs concentrated on her erstwhile protector. That's what a sensible person would do.

With a flash of insight, Janie realized she could not wait for police intervention to arrive, nor could she abandon a man who had risked so much for her sake. Those kinds of people were too rare, too special. It didn't matter whether he was really a cop or not, although she believed he was. The important element was survival. And right now his chances didn't look promising.

She inched her car past a couple of stopped vehicles whose occupants were leaning out windows, aiming phones at the scene to take pictures despite the obvious risk. Didn't they think? Didn't they care how close they were to possible harm or even death?

Well, *she* did. But that wasn't going to stop her. Silent prayer formed the background for her actions as she completed the final turn and aimed her compact car toward the crumpled pickup truck. It wasn't too late to change her mind and flee, she reasoned.

"No. No. No," Janie said over and over, the volume of her voice rising with each repetition.

Her engine roared, tires whining as they slipped on the pavement seeking traction. Pixie joined the chorus of sound with a high-pitched howl.

Janie gripped the steering wheel like a drowning person would a lifeline and charged into the standoff. The armed men didn't take their eyes off Brad so she honked her horn in a long blast they couldn't ignore.

The closest man turned, weapon in hand. Janie swerved toward him.

He dived clear, landing on a grassy verge.

The second man emerged from behind the SUV, took aim at Janie's car as she passed and fired. The rear window shattered into a thousand tiny pieces.

Ducking, she peeked over the dash only enough to make sure she didn't run over Brad.

He was limping into the middle of the street and waving his arms while bystanders took cover behind closed doors.

"Get in," she shouted, skidding to a stop beside him.

Visible anger wasn't enough to keep him from opening the door and throwing himself onto the seat. She was already moving before he got both feet in and managed to slam the door.

"What was that?" Brad demanded.

"Just returning a favor," Janie yelled back, taking the closest corner on two wheels and barely missing several vehicles of lookie-loos who were scattering after hearing the gunshot.

The narrow escape had left her elated enough to start to grin. She glanced over at him as she straightened the wheel and accelerated. "We made it!"

Brad's eye roll and expression of disgust struck her so funny she laughed.

When he said, "I can't believe you actually did that," Janie agreed.

"I can't believe I did, either."

FOUR

Brad stayed on edge until he was certain they had temporarily evaded their pursuers. Janie had wisely taken to the back roads of Springfield and seemed to be relaxing a little, too, except for the death grip she had on her steering wheel.

"I think we're in the clear," he said. "See if you can find a secluded place to pull over."

"Why?" Her eyes were wide as she glanced his way.

"Because it's time I filled you in about what's been going on."

"It can't be as scary as what my imagination has come up with," Janie quipped with a nervous laugh.

"Don't count on it." Brad was sorry

she'd become involved but, thinking back, he couldn't see how he could have prevented it.

"Okay." She wheeled into the driveway of a house whose yard was unkempt and cluttered with trash. There was a dilapidated for-sale sign nailed to a tree fronting the street. "How about here?"

"This will do as long as we leave the car and step into the shadows."

Janie huffed as she climbed out and checked the condition of her faithful car. "Why bother? The bullet hole in what's left of the window kind of stands out."

Scooping up a handful of soggy leaves, Brad scattered them over the trunk lid, distracting from the damage. "That will help disguise it." He dusted off his palms and reached for her hand. "Come with me."

"No way."

He was about to insist when Janie opened the rear door of her sedan, bent for a few seconds, then lifted a squirming little mop of a dog into her arms. "I'm not leaving Pixie."

"Fine. Bring her. Just get out of sight before somebody sees us. As a matter of fact…" He reached in and grabbed the small duffel containing the drug shipment. "I'll take this with us, too. No sense tempting fate."

"I don't believe in fate or luck," Janie countered. "I believe in God."

"Yeah." Brad shrugged. "Me, too, but I also know how badly humans can mess up their lives by making foolish decisions." He turned to lead the way through the wet knee-high grass and into what had apparently been a cozy backyard.

Despite the puddles of rainwater, Janie snapped a short, pink leash on Pixie's collar and let her down to sniff around where someone or something had flattened an area of the grass.

"Watch out for feral dogs and cats," Brad warned. "That little pup is barely a mouthful for whatever lives back here."

"She'd bark if there was something dangerous around," Janie said with conviction. "Okay. We're out of sight. What did you want to talk to me about?"

Brad raked his fingers through his dark hair. "Me. And this mess we're in," he said. "I told you I was working undercover, right?"

"So you said. I take it there are illegal drugs in that bag of yours you seem so fond of."

"Not fond. And not mine," he replied. "I was assigned to infiltrate a low-level tier of a widespread smuggling operation in the hopes I could get a line on the so-called honest businessmen who actually pull all the strings. Everything was going smoothly until Tim Speevey got shot." He began to pace the small area. "I couldn't just let him die. It's not in me. I tried to help him on my own, then finally convinced his father to take him to the hospital."

"Where you met me."

"Yes." Shaking his head slowly he sought empathy in her eyes. What he saw was more akin to distrust. "I never meant for the old man or Bubba to come in with me. I was just going to drop Tim off and trust him to professional care."

"But the man wanted to stay with his wounded son."

Brad nodded. "Yeah. You know the rest."

"Not all of it," Janie said. "For instance, I don't know why you called to warn me or how those men in the SUV found either of us." She paused. "Well?"

He shrugged, arms out, palms up. "Warning you was the right thing to do. Speevey was furious about Bubba and said he was going to take it out on you. As soon as he and a couple of new thugs left me and headed for the hospital, I tried to call my chief and have him order protection. When I couldn't get through to speak to him privately, I phoned you." Brad peered around the closest corner of the house, checking the street and seeing no problems. "It's a good thing I did or these guys might have caught you at home and we wouldn't be having this conversation."

Shafts of filtered sunlight glittered off raindrops as well as off the moisture in her expressive eyes. He'd have had to be blindfolded to miss the emotion, the vulnerability. Nevertheless, Janie stood with her chin up, shoulders back. In his opinion, this emergency room nurse was as spunky as her little dog. And would be just as ineffective in a gun battle.

"Okay, so let's go to the police," Janie said. "You can turn over the bag of drugs and I can report that I've been followed."

"Two problems with that," Brad said flatly. "One, I don't want to reveal who I am and ruin weeks of undercover work. The way I see it, I still have a shot at completing my mission."

"What's the second problem?"

"Deciding who to trust. That's why so few people know what I'm doing. As nearly as we can tell, my chief's teenage son, Wesley Jr., was gunned down on the street by somebody who discovered who he was related to. He was less criminal than he was stupid but that didn't matter. He'd written his dad a letter, explaining why he was in trouble and asking for help, but he was killed before the chief could get to him. We know which syndicate he was dealing with. We just don't know who the real moneymen are. If we take down the street criminals, the others may escape punishment. That's not what we want."

"I get it. I really do," Janie said. She bent to scoop up Pixie and hold her close despite wet paws. "You don't want to go to the authorities yet. But what's to keep me from doing that?"

"Being believed comes to mind," Brad said. "All you can prove is that someone shot at you. The rest is nothing but your word against the opinion of anybody who doesn't buy your story. Lots of citizens think they're being stalked when they're not. You need solid proof."

"How about the bullet hole in my car?" Her voice was rising.

"The chief's son, Wesley, had a fatal

bullet in *him* and his death was ruled a simple drive-by. That's one of the reasons I undertook this assignment. To prove otherwise."

"You have an excuse for anything that will get you your way, don't you?"

The phone in Brad's pocket began to ring. Raising a hand to quiet her, he pulled it out and answered, "Yeah?"

The shouting from his caller made him hold the phone away from his ear. Janie's eyebrows arched as she stared. Brad waited until the epithets ceased before he said, "I'm right here, Mr. Speevey. Not to worry. I took the shipment with me for safekeeping."

"Well, bring it back."

"Um, gladly. No problem. Where are you?"

Although Brad was listening to his cell he was watching Janie. She began to shake her head vigorously and mouth, *No!* over and over again.

"My truck got wrecked so I'll have to

grab a car off somebody. It may take me a little while to get back to you."

The connection was once again filled with incoherent yelling and name-calling. Then Brad heard what sounded like a scuffle and all grew quiet. "Hello?"

The voice that replaced that of the frantic old man was calm, deep and menacing. "Where are you?"

"Better yet, who are you?" Brad asked.

"You dented my buddy's SUV. That's all you need to know."

"That was just a misunderstanding." Hoping he sounded a lot more confident than he felt, Brad bluffed. "The real problem is Speevey's going off the rails because of his boys. You and I both know that."

"And?"

"And I'll be glad to deliver the goods. I just don't want to turn anything over to that unstable old man. No telling what he's said about me, you know?"

"What do you propose?"

"An exchange in public. Someplace

where we have plenty of witnesses, just in case."

"In case of what?"

Brad faked a laugh. "In case you guys don't believe I'm on your side. I promise, I only made off with the bag because I wasn't sure what Speevey was going to do next. Were you listening when he started making threats?"

The answer was a nonanswer but Brad had to accept it when the caller said, "All right. Where are you?"

"Pretty far north and on foot, thanks to your pals. What do you say to meeting at the downtown Springfield Sportsman's Complex, maybe over in the section where they sell the speed boats?"

"When?"

"First thing tomorrow morning."

"No good. Today."

Steeling himself for a meeting that could too easily result in his death, Brad nevertheless agreed. "Okay. But like I said, it will take me a while to get there."

"What about the woman I heard picked you up after the wreck?"

"She chickened out and dumped me," Brad said, wishing it was true. "Like I told Speevey, I have to boost a car before I can drive back into town."

"Okay. Be there by seven."

"How about ten instead?"

"I thought you wanted the exchange to take place in a crowd."

"Yeah, yeah. I do. Okay. Seven, it is. How will I find you? That's a lot of boats."

"Don't worry," the thug said, "we'll find you."

Janie stared as Brad ended the call. "You have to be kidding. You can't face the same bunch of guys who already tried to kill us."

"I have to."

"And you called that poor old man nuts." Janie made a face.

"This is my job. But it's not yours. Here's where we part company, Ms. Kirkpatrick."

"In a pig's eye we do. I'm not going to let you steal some innocent person's car just to keep a rendezvous with a bullet. I'll drive you."

"No."

"Yes. End of discussion. You've already saved me multiple times, starting years ago when you intervened on my behalf with my abusive brothers, not to mention keeping me from being shot in the emergency room."

"The hospital fiasco was my fault. I owed it to you."

"Don't make excuses." She made a face and shook her head. "Some people are breakers and some are menders. It's their nature. You're a mender like me. You'd have tried to protect me even if we'd been enemies. Come on. Admit it." Pausing, she waited for him to agree with her. To her surprise, it didn't take long.

"What if I would have? That doesn't change anything. I'm still trying to do the right thing and keep you out of trouble."

Janie felt the beginnings of a smile and

let it blossom. "So am I. And that includes helping you as much as I can. I don't see it as returning the favor, I see it as my duty. Nursing is the same thing for me. It's my job to use my knowledge and skill for the benefit of others. Period. Face it, Brad, our motivations are very similar. Would you back off and let me go solo if I were in your place? Would you?"

It was easy to see how frustrated he was becoming even before he spoke. "There's no comparison. I'm trained as a police officer and did a stint in the army. You're on the side that patches up other people's mistakes."

"Same thing."

"Hah! No way."

Clearly, the stubborn man wasn't grasping her point. Okay. If there was nothing she could say that would convince him, she'd have to take matters into her own hands. What she wanted to do was wrest the bag of drugs away from him and go straight to the police but she didn't see how that was possible. Her second choice was to leave him to his own devices and pray that no innocents were harmed. *Innocents like me*, Janie added to herself.

She turned, clutched Pixie to her chest and started to walk back around the corner of the deserted house. She didn't have to look behind to feel certain Brad was following. That sense was reinforced when she stopped abruptly and he bumped into her back, his momentum almost knocking her down.

Gasping, Janie faltered. Brad caught her and kept her upright. She bit back a louder cry. His strong arms encircled her, pulling her out of sight.

"In—in the street," she managed to choke out.

When Brad positioned her against the outer wall and stepped back he didn't order her to stay. He didn't have to. Doing so was instinctive.

He put his index finger to his lips. "Quiet."

Her nod was rapid and unmistakable.

No way was she going to move, other than trembling, given what she'd seen passing by.

Brad left her and circled the opposite side of the abandoned structure, leaving prints in the wet grass as his shoes and pant legs drew moisture.

Janie waited a few long seconds, then tiptoed after him. When she touched his shoulder he jumped a foot, then rounded on her. "I told you to stay back."

"Not in so many words, you didn't," Janie argued. "Did you see the same car I did? It was cruising by really slowly."

"Yes." He backed up, shoving her farther into the shadows of overgrown bushes.

"*Now* are you going to let me help you?"

"Yes, and no. I don't want you running into our friends by yourself so we'll stay together a little longer. We'll still need to ditch your car for something less obvious."

"I refuse to ride in a stolen vehicle."

"Aargh!" Brad rolled his eyes, clearly on the verge of shouting. Well, too bad. She had principles, even if his undercover work had corrupted him to the point of behaving like one of the criminals he was pitted against.

"You're going to have to make an exception unless you want your next ride to be in an ambulance."

Janie huffed. "I'm surprised you didn't say *hearse*."

"I thought of it."

"No doubt. You need to remember which side of the law you're supposed to be on, Mr. Undercover Officer. There must be a way to accomplish a change of cars without stealing one."

To her relief he nodded. "There is. If I can get through to my chief he'll be able to help." As he started to reach for her upper arms again, Pixie intercepted one finger and bit down.

Brad jumped away, shaking his hand from the wrist. "Ouch! What did she do that for? She was friendly before."

"That was when you and I were getting along," Janie told him. "Keep acting like my enemy and she'll keep defending me."

"Then I wish she was a lot bigger and meaner," he said with a grimace. "Just between you and me, our chances of getting out of this while we're still together are slim and none. Believe me, you *don't* want to stay involved with me."

"I thought you said you needed to protect me."

"I did. I do. But not forever." Shouldering past her, Brad peered into the street again. "The coast looks clear. Come on. We need to move before that car comes back by."

No way was Janie going to argue with that. Keeping pace she jogged behind him to her car and started to open the driver's door.

Brad pushed her aside. "I'm driving."

"I don't think so." As she was speaking she noticed his attention shift. That caused her to mimic his focus. A car exactly like the one she'd seen was turning the corner. Coming toward them. And they were exposed this time.

In one fluid motion, Brad jerked open

the rear door and shoved her and the little dog inside, then slid behind the wheel. He reached for the ignition.

Anticipating his command, Janie pulled a key ring from the pocket of her jeans and slapped it into his extended hand at the same time he was shouting, "Key!"

Janie ducked, covering and shielding Pixie.

Brad bent to find the slot and insert the key.

The engine sputtered, then caught. Tires slipped and screeched as he reversed out of the driveway.

Janie held on tightly. Her car skidded in a semicircle, coming to rest facing the approaching vehicle.

Brad shouted, "Hang on!" and floored the gas.

FIVE

Racing past the approaching SUV, Brad was unable to determine if a regular citizen or a thug was behind the wheel. Taking no chances, he continued to drive defensively until he could be certain nobody was on their trail.

As he slowed he saw Janie raise up to peer over the top of the seat.

"We lost them. For now," Brad said with as much conviction as he could muster. "I'll pull over and you can come up front with me."

"Don't stop. I'll crawl over the seat," Janie replied. She began by placing Pixie into the canvas carrier, then flinging one leg over the back of the passenger-side bucket seat.

"Just don't kick me, okay?"

"You mean accidentally, right?"

He snorted a wry chuckle. "Whatever. I managed to ditch that car pretty easily. That worries me."

"Why? Maybe it was just an innocent passerby."

"That, or it may mean that the guys Speevey alerted have split up. There's probably more than one chase vehicle and they hope to box us in. Keep your eyes peeled."

"Oh, terrific. Just what I wanted to hear."

"Hey, you're the one who insisted on staying with me."

"And you agreed."

"Under duress," Brad grumbled back at her. "Keep your head down no matter where you're sitting, at least until I've managed to contact Chief Winterhaven and come up with a plan."

"What can he do for us? He's way up in KC, right?"

Brad chose to ignore her reference to

them as a team. "He has personal connections all over the state. I intend to ask him for a different car—and I'd appreciate you not hollering in the background about your lofty principles."

"In other words, theft was all your idea."

"You have a problem with that?"

"Yes. But I'm good as long as you don't make me guilty by association."

"I'd explain everything in the long run and make restitution, you know. You wouldn't be blamed. And nobody would be hurt."

Janie had scrunched down in the seat as far as the safety belt would allow, her arms crossed, knees bent. *Small person, small target*, Brad thought. *Good.*

She blew a noisy sigh. "Then you'd better not go and get yourself killed or I'll never forgive you."

"What tender sentiments." Brad had to chuckle. "I can see why you make such an empathetic caregiver. You have a real connection to the problems of others and soothe them with your kind words."

"You're special," she said with evident sarcasm. "I save only my sweetest expressions for you."

That comment made him laugh more despite their tenuous situation. "You don't fool me," he countered. "Behind that steely persona is a heart of mush." The gaze he turned on her mirrored that conclusion and he could tell she was moved.

Perhaps treating her gently wasn't the smartest choice. When she was good and angry her fight-or-flight reactions were keenest. Plus, Brad was starting to have more and more trouble with his personal opinion of the spunky nurse. He liked her. Truly liked her. And his admiration for both her courage and strong moral character kept boosting his concern as well as making him edgy.

The more he cared about Janie Kirkpatrick, he concluded, the more vulnerable he would be. He must not allow himself to become careless simply because his thoughts had strayed to Janie instead of staying focused on his job.

Brad gritted his teeth as he cast a side-long glance at her. She must have noticed the subtle movement of his head because she met his gaze. There were unshed tears in her eyes, yet her expression held promise. Hope. In spite of—or perhaps because of—her dysfunctional upbringing, she was resilient no matter what life threw at her.

That was what he envied, Brad decided. What he wanted to learn from her. She stood firm against the kinds of experiences that could bring almost anyone down. When he'd been given the undercover assignment he'd approached it in a workmanlike manner, knowing what to do and moving forward. But he hadn't had an unquestionable conviction that he would succeed.

In his place, with equal training and experience, he knew Janie Kirkpatrick would have been positive of her success. And, by virtue of her mere presence, she was giving him more hope.

That was crazy. It was also true and

would bear further analysis later, when nobody was trying to catch and perhaps kill them. With only half of his mind on the problem at hand, Brad swung into the immense parking lot surrounding the sports complex that took up several city blocks right in the midst of Springfield.

"Aren't we way too early?" Janie asked.

"For the rendezvous about the drug exchange, yes," Brad said. He drove the aisles until he'd found a tight spot between two trucks. "We'll leave your car here and hope we won't have to come back to it, so take all your personal property with you." He nodded toward the back seat. "The guard dog, too. Isn't there somebody in town you can park her with until the threat is neutralized?"

"I—I don't have many friends outside the hospital. I suppose we could take her there and I could ask around."

Brad quirked a smile. "Why am I getting the idea you don't really want to part with that dog?"

"Intuitive as well as strong and handsome," Janie said. "My, my."

"Flattery will get you nowhere, lady."

"Okay, then, speaking of the hospital, how about a little common sense? Tim Speevey may be so medicated for the pain that he's more likely to talk. Why don't we go ask him some questions while we can? I can get you in."

"He should have a guard posted outside his room. I don't want to take the chance I'll be recognized."

"Then you can tell me what to ask and I'll talk to him alone."

"No, you won't."

Janie was grinning. "That's what I figured you'd say. So, are we going to sit here like targets in a carnival shooting gallery or are we going to do something creative? Think out of the box?"

Arching his eyebrows over dark eyes, Brad stared at her. "In spite of my misgivings about trying to see Tim, I have to admit it may be a good idea."

"Wonder of wonders!"

"Don't get smug. I'll put in a call to my chief about getting us a different car and then we'll try to sneak back to the hospital. It stands to reason that nobody will expect you to do that."

"Hopefully," Janie said quietly.

Brad wanted to at least pat the back of her hand, if not hug her for encouragement, but he refrained. They had enough confusion running rampant between them without adding unnecessary shows of affection.

"You keep watch while I make the call," Brad ordered, trying to sound gruff and succeeding more than he'd intended. "And while we're together, turn off your own phone, just in case they're tracking it."

Janie gave him a mock salute, then turned her attention to the surrounding parking lot. He could tell she was edgy yet hiding her fear extremely well. Good. He wanted her ultra-alert. A frightened watchman was bound to be most vigilant.

Brad just hoped and prayed she wouldn't spot anything dangerous. Planning to change phones as soon as possible, he lifted his cell and called his chief.

"What did he say?" Janie asked as they drove toward the hospital, still in her damaged car. It was all she could do to keep from fidgeting. As it was, her hands were clasped tightly together.

"He'll have a new pickup truck waiting for us when we go back to the sports complex later. We can find it by the GPS coordinates he's sending as soon as it's in place."

"Very high-tech. I'm impressed."

"You should be."

She decided to press him more since he seemed to be amenable to answering. "So, with all this computer stuff and technical help, why did you need to go undercover? I mean, if he can reach all over the state via the web, why can't the chief figure out who the bosses of the crime ring are?"

"We have plenty of good ideas and names of possible suspects," Brad replied. "What we need is proof. Somebody ordered Wesley Jr. killed. That's the man we really want to pin down. The rest is incidental."

"Incidental? They're acting pretty *lethal* if you ask me."

"A lot depends on viewpoint. Mine is necessarily narrowed. You're seeing it all at once. No wonder it's confusing and scary."

Janie rolled her eyes below arching brows. "If I was reading this in a mystery novel, I wouldn't believe it."

"I don't know why not. The bullets were plenty real."

"It's the background details you gave me that make no sense. Why would wealthy men be involved in something so shady? They're already rolling in money."

"Which may or may not be dirty. Why do you think they call it laundering money when it's reinvested to mask its origins? If we could trace it all, we'd probably be amazed."

"I already am," Janie told him, falling silent as the familiar streets flew by. So far, so good. She'd had a few sightings of dark SUVs but those had held normal drivers—people just going about daily mundane business.

The approach to the hospital caused her breathing to speed, her palms to perspire despite the cold, damp wind blowing in through the broken window. "Visiting hours are about to end but unless you plan to stay here for a long time, I recommend you park where most of the other cars are." She pointed. "Back up to the side of the helipad so the broken window isn't so noticeable."

To her surprise, Brad didn't argue. He merely followed directions, then handed her the ignition key. "Here. Take this. And stuff that bag of drugs under the seat so it isn't visible."

Janie's brow knit. "I thought you wanted to drive."

"I did. I do. You hold the car key. If something happens to me, get out of here as fast as you can and go to the cops, like you wanted."

She refused to even consider losing him. "Don't be silly. Nothing is going to happen to you. As long as you stick with me we'll be in and out in a flash. We have to be. I don't want to leave poor Pixie alone for very long."

The wry smile he showed her was better than words at expressing doubt. Janie could understand his misgivings. She was having them, too. Big-time. Yet she was convinced her plan was a good one. After all, he was going along with it so it must not be too off-the-wall.

Leading the way, she climbed the concrete ramp next to the emergency room doors and straight-armed her way inside. Chances were the ER docs had put Tim in the ICU. Although, to make it easier to guard him, it was possible he had a private room.

She put out an arm to halt Brad's progress. "Wait here. I'll go find out where your buddy is and come back for you."

"Promise?"

"I just gave you my word."

He shook his head and raked his fingers through his wavy hair, obviously frustrated. "Yeah. You did. I guess I've been spending too much time with people who lie."

"Well, hopefully that will soon end," she said softly as she lightly touched his forearm. Compassion filled her. So did a plethora of confusing emotions. Years ago she had vowed to never trust another man, likening them all to her father and brothers, and she'd never before been this close to changing her mind.

It's because of the element of risk, Janie insisted. That had to be it. She and Brad had been thrust into a firestorm of danger and forced to rely upon each other, that was all. Once she could return to her former life and stop worrying about assassins, the appeal of Brad's company would wane.

A shiver shot up her spine and she pivoted to check her surroundings as she hurried to the first-floor nurses' station.

No one was present so she circled the

counter, typed her code into the computer and called up Tim Speevey's record. He'd been put on the second floor. If she led Brad up the stairway instead of taking the elevator, they could access Tim's room quickly and quietly.

Janie was almost running as she returned to the entrance where she'd left her temporary ally. She rounded the corner. Skidded to a stop. Gasped.

Brad was gone!

SIX

A black SUV had cruised past Janie's parked car twice before Brad decided to try to get a closer look at it. And make sure the people inside weren't going for the drugs he'd left hidden beneath the seat.

Because he'd checked the hallway and hadn't spotted Janie coming back, he figured he'd have enough time to record the license number before she missed him. Keeping to the side of the exit, he was partially hidden by the arrival of an ambulance. The crew backed it into the bay, parked and began cleaning and restocking medical supplies.

That diversion helped. Brad saw the black car a third time. It slowed to check out the ambulance crew, then inched out

of sight, giving him time to memorize several digits of the Missouri license on the rear bumper.

Not totally satisfied, he was thinking about lingering when the door behind him flew open. He ducked and whirled. Janie! He was so breathless she might as well have punched him in the stomach.

"I thought you were going to wait for me," she shouted. "Is this all your promises are worth? You scared me to death!"

Brad joined her in two long steps, grasped her arms and tried to reason with her. "Shush. You're attracting attention."

"Well, duh. You could have tried—"

That was all he permitted before silencing her with a kiss.

Wrapping her in a close embrace, he threaded his fingers through her hair. To Brad's surprise, she quit fighting him. Her arms slipped around him. She was kissing him back. As he braced himself against the wall of the ambulance bay, he heard snickering in the background. Obviously, the EMTs were enjoying the impromptu kiss as much as he was.

Which was patently wrong, Brad told himself. He hadn't meant the display of affection to be genuine, yet it had morphed into the kind of kiss most people only dream of.

Janie was breathless as he straightened and leaned away. Her blue eyes glistened and her soft lips were trembling. Taking stock of his own feelings, he had to admit he wasn't in much better shape.

"Sorry," Brad whispered, drawing an unsteady breath. "I had to shut you up."

She swallowed hard, yet failed to release her hold on him. "W-why?"

He glanced over his shoulder, not expecting to see the SUV. Instead of making another pass, however, it had pulled into a recently vacated parking spot.

Keeping one arm around her waist, Brad hustled her back inside. "Your car may have been spotted."

She tried to peer past him. He stopped her. "Don't look. They're just getting out of their car. You may as well take me to Tim's room until I'm sure the coast is clear outside."

"Second floor," she managed to squeak out.

Brad started toward a bank of elevators.

Janie slipped aside, grasped his hand and tugged. "No. Stairs. Follow me."

He didn't argue. She knew the hospital ins and outs and he didn't. Only a fool would have disagreed with her.

Only a fool would have kissed her, he told himself, still reeling from the experience. If she had been nearly as emotionally affected as he had, they had a real problem. And it was his fault.

But what a kiss! he thought, awed. *Wow.*

Following her into a stairwell, Brad gladly kept hold of her hand. It was warm and soft, yet her grip was stronger than he had expected. Remembering how she had so easily flipped Bubba, he began to realize this nurse wasn't nearly as helpless as he'd first assumed. That was a plus—as long as she didn't try to pit martial arts skills against a gun or a knife.

His fingers instinctively squeezed hers as they climbed and he saw her cheeks grow pinker. She paused on the second-floor landing, her free hand on the bar that unlatched the closed stairway.

The look she gave him at that moment reflected some of the fondness he was feeling. At least he imagined it did. "Just tell me which way to go and you can stay here, out of sight," Brad said.

"I'd rather be with you." Janie reached into her pocket and palmed a plastic card with her picture and a bar code imprinted on it. "If you run into a guard or another nurse you'll need my badge to get past them."

He knew she was right. So why was he having so much trouble agreeing?

Silently, still holding hands, she pushed open the door and they stepped into the hallway together. At one end, where the hall turned a corner, a uniformed police officer was sipping soda from a can. At the other end, elevator doors were opening and closing.

Brad took the lead. "Okay. Come on. See if you can get us past the cop in the hall."

"It would be better if I were wearing scrubs," Janie said.

"Then let's get some."

Her eyes widened. "Right. This way."

A supply room door unlocked in response to her pass card. She ducked inside, pulling him along with her. It didn't escape Brad's notice that they were very much alone and he hoped she didn't want another kiss because he wasn't sure he'd be able to deny her.

Janie's businesslike movements made him laugh at himself. There was no subterfuge for him to resist. She merely handed him a white lab coat and said, "Put that on," while she donned a blue, pullover top, then turned to size him up.

"You need a stethoscope," Janie told him. "If we can't find one lying around, a clipboard will probably suffice. Do you happen to have a comb on you?"

"Um, no." He raked fingers through his longish hair.

"Then here," she said. "Bend down so I can tie this surgical cap."

"I'll look silly."

"No sillier than any real doctor looks," she countered, putting her plan into motion. "Better."

"What else?" Brad asked.

That brought the first smile he'd seen from her in a long time. "Look superior and aloof."

He chuckled. "You don't like doctors?"

"Some of them are great," she replied. "Others? Well…"

"Okay. I get it. I'm the smart-aleck kind."

"Right." Her smile grew lopsided. "Pretend."

Approaching the guard at Tim's door, Janie forced herself to act calm and in control when her heart was actually about to pound out of her chest.

She flashed her ID card and tilted her head toward Brad, who was cradling the clipboard she'd given him. "The doctor needs to check on his patient."

Saluting with the soda can, the guard nodded. "Have at it, Doc."

Janie replied, "Thanks," then stood back to let Brad enter the private room ahead of her. She didn't realize she'd been holding her breath until the door shut behind them.

Tim lay in the only occupied bed, his eyes closed. His bronzed complexion was sallow, yet when Janie checked, his pulse was strong. She lifted one of his eyelids. "Out like a light. They must have given him painkillers."

"Any way you can wake him?"

"I can try." She leaned closer to the injured man's ear and called his name. "Tim? Tim, can you hear me? Open your eyes."

Although his lids fluttered, he didn't answer. She touched his shoulder through the hospital gown. "Hey, Tim! Wake up."

Shaking her head as she straightened,

Janie looked to Brad. "I'm sorry. He's deep. If I knew what they'd given him and how long ago, I'd be able to make a fair prediction of when he'd stir. As it is, I have no idea."

Brad scowled. "Can't you look it up?"

"If I had access to the computer records system here in the room, I could. The days of hanging paper charts at the end of a patient's bed are pretty much in the past."

"Best guess?" Brad had circled to the opposite side of the bed. Janie didn't like the way he was studying the patient.

"No guess," she answered quickly. "The only safe way to bring him out of it is with reversal drugs and I don't have access."

"You can't get them or you won't."

"Same thing," Janie insisted. "If I gave him the wrong meds, I could kill him."

"Okay, okay." Brad began to pace. His path took him to the window and he looked down on the parking area. "The car I was worried about is still there. We can't leave yet. Not safely."

"Well, we can't stay in here, either,"

Janie argued. "Nurses will be in to check Tim's condition and a real doctor may actually show up, too."

"Plus, we need to be back at the rendezvous site soon."

She pulled a face. "Don't remind me."

"So, where can we hide until that car leaves?"

"Don't look at me. I got you this far but I don't have some clever plan to get us back out." Frustration and concern filled Janie's mind. She supposed they could return to the storage closet but that idea was far from foolproof. Others visited the various staff-only areas regularly.

"Maybe we can…" Janie began, cutting off midsentence when she heard a strange sound outside the closed door to Tim's room. She and Brad both stared at the door. Anyone who had ever dropped a half-empty soft drink can would have recognized the tinny clink of it hitting the hard floor.

The guard! Janie cast around for someplace to hide, deciding on the gathered

curtain at one side of the empty second
bed. Brad dived for the bathroom and
eased its door shut just as the room door
swung open.

Janie tried to breathe silently. Her feet
were next to a movable bed table and the
curtain stopped at her knees so if anyone happened to be checking the room
she knew she could be spotted. Why, oh
why, hadn't she followed Brad into the
bathroom? Too late now.

Mumbled voices were hard to make
out but she could tell that more than one
man had entered and proceeded to Tim's
bed. The urge to peek out was strong. So
was the desire to stay hidden. Given the
abrupt entry and the sound of the dropped
can, she had to assume the interlopers had
eliminated the guard. They definitely
weren't medical staff.

"Now," one of them said a little louder.

Janie tensed. Tried to see through the
folds of the heavy curtain with poor re-
sults. She looked sideways and caught
a hazy reflection in the glass section of

the door. At least two burly men dressed in black T-shirts and jeans were bending over the patient while a third stood guard. She bit her lip to keep from crying out or racing to Tim's aid. There was no way she could be certain that her martial arts training would be sufficient to disable three thugs no matter how strongly she wished it would. If only Brad was where she could speak to him, work out a plan of attack.

In seconds the men at Tim's bedside turned to leave. One of them tossed aside a pillow. Janie covered her mouth to stifle a gasp. She fingered the edge of the curtain and stared toward the bathroom door as it glided open.

Brad beat her to the bed by a second or two. He was already checking Tim's pulse when she joined him and lifted one of the patient's eyelids again. This time, the pupils were large and dilated, his eyes unresponsive to light.

"They killed him," she whispered.

"Looks like it." He grasped her arm and

pulled her toward the exit. "There was no way we could have stopped them without dying, too. Come on. We have to get out of here before somebody thinks we're responsible."

A puddle of light brown soda was oozing beneath the door as Brad eased it open slightly. Janie jerked away to check the prone body of the policeman. "He's still breathing. Pulse is strong," she reported. "I have to get him help."

"Look around us," Brad said, sounding forceful if panicky. "There's plenty of aid on the way."

"Right, but—"

"No buts," he said. "If I have to sling you over my shoulder and carry you out of here, I will."

Making a snap decision she reached for his extended hand, let him pull her to her feet and ran with him down the hallway as others raced past to aid the downed officer. Brad was right, yet she was also still a nurse. A good one.

And one in trouble up to her neck, she

concluded as they pounded back down the stairs.

She would have burst from the stair-well on the ground floor if Brad had not stopped her. He jerked his chin toward the lobby where the three large men in black clothing were making for the automatic exit doors. That gave her a better look at one of their faces and fair profile images of the other two. All were giving off vibes of warning, causing others to back off as if a wave of enmity was sweeping through with them.

"Do you recognize anybody?" Janie asked Brad in a whisper.

"I think the tallest one was with Speevey at the motel," he answered. "I'm not sure about the other two."

"My shoes are sticky. I must have stepped in the spilled soda by Tim's room. They'll know I was there!"

"Hopefully, the unconscious guard will ID the guys who hit him and we won't be blamed."

"You can guarantee that?" Watching

him roll his eyes she realized that was a foolish question. Every move they made was being thwarted and she was getting discouraged, big-time.

Janie's shoulders slumped as she sighed. "Okay. What's next?"

"We see if they recognized your car. I think, if they had, they'd have stayed to watch for us. They're driving away."

"They are?" Her spirits lifted. "We can go now?"

Brad nodded as he checked his cell phone. "Yes. I've received the GPS coordinates of our new car—actually, it's a truck like my wrecked one—and we need to go pick it up." He palmed her keys. "You can drive while I phone a progress report to Chief Winterhaven."

"Well, I hope he comes up with a better plan than we've done lately."

To her shock, Brad flashed a grin. He pushed through the door and started for the parking lot, clearly satisfied that their enemies had gone.

Janie wasn't convinced. Looking furtively back and forth she followed him until he reached for her and drew her to his side.

"If that's your idea of being nonchalant, we are in deep trouble," he quipped. "Come on. Smile. Relax. You look scared witless."

"I am. I was in the same room where a man was murdered and found a policeman assaulted. How can I act as if I don't care?"

"Caring is fine. I'd expect no less of you. It's letting your emotions affect your outward behavior that will sink us if we reveal too much."

She felt him give her a quick squeeze. It buoyed her spirits some. So did comprehending what he was asking of her.

"You want me to pretend I'm fine the same way I did when my brothers hit me and my father was so drunk he didn't care. Is that it?"

When Brad looked down at her, Janie lifted her chin in defiance. "I get it. And I can do it because I will never forget how

I was treated." After a short pause she added, "Just don't expect me to like the way it makes me feel or the memories it brings back."

SEVEN

Brad guided Janie by acting as if they were a couple and keeping her close to his side. He could tell she was anything but relaxed. As he'd told her, that didn't matter nearly as much as putting on a good show for anyone who happened to be watching.

They were circling the building, heading for the far reaches of the parking lot, when he heard someone calling Janie's name. "Ignore her," Brad ordered.

"But I wouldn't do that. Ever." She pulled away from him enough to glance over her shoulder. "It's just one of the other nurses going on duty. Nothing to worry about."

"Unless she tells the police or hospital security that she saw us leaving together."

"I didn't think of that. Sorry." Janie scowled. "And stop looking at me like that."

"Like what?"

"Like you think I'm dumber than dirt."

Brad was taken aback. "I wasn't doing that. You're one of the smartest women I've ever met."

"But?"

"But you're also too naive. You don't think like a criminal."

"I'll take that as a compliment."

He let go as she slid behind the wheel of her car, then circled to the passenger side and climbed in. "It wasn't meant to be favorable."

"Nevertheless." Janie was frowning as she started the engine and put the car in gear. "Before we do anything else I want to check on Pixie. She's too quiet."

Brad huffed. "I was just thinking how peaceful it was without all that yipping." He got to his knees and leaned over the back of the front seat to reach the carrying case. "Just drive. I'll get the mutt out for you. Hopefully, she won't bite me again."

The car was moving. He began to unzip the case, fully expecting a little black button nose to poke out. It didn't.

"Is she okay?" Janie asked.

"Hang on."

Brad pulled the zipper all the way around and threw open the top flap. His heart dropped. There was no dog inside.

Without comment he turned back and slid down into the seat, then reached forward to locate the bag of drugs they'd stashed beneath the seat. Wonder of wonders, it was still there.

"What?" Janie demanded.

"Pull over."

"What is it? Has something happened to Pixie?"

As soon as she undid her seat belt she bolted out of the car and yanked open the rear door. Brad saw her jaw drop when she saw the empty carrier.

"Simmer down," he said, trying to effect

calm. "She has to be in here somewhere. Maybe she's hiding."

"No, they took her. They must have."

By this time he was beside her. "I don't think so. The drugs are still here. They wouldn't take your dog and leave a valuable shipment behind."

"Then where is she?"

"I don't know. Help me look."

Tears were cascading down Janie's cheeks and her hands were shaking. She dropped to her knees beside the car and leaned in, peering beneath the seats. Brad did the same at the front, then released the catch on the trunk and looked in there, too. Clearly, the little mop of a dog was gone.

"You locked the car, didn't you?" Janie asked between ragged breaths.

"Of course I did." Unless she had inadvertently unlocked it when he'd handed her the keys. It was such a remote possibility he decided to keep the notion to himself. This was no time to place blame. "Maybe she jumped out the broken window."

"Oh, no!"

Brad took charge. "Look. You're too upset to get behind the wheel. Climb in and watch for her while I drive."

"No! I'm not leaving here without my dog."

"Yes, you are. We both are." Watching her slowly back away from him gave Brad bad vibes.

Janie spun on her heel and took off running across the parking lot. Rather than chase her on foot, Brad decided to use the car so that they could flee together as soon as he caught up to her. She cut the corner by the side of the L-shaped hospital annex, slipping on damp ground cover. He could hear her screaming for her dog as if a wolf pack was pursuing them.

While keeping an eye out for the little white dog, Brad rolled down the car's windows and cruised slowly, cautiously, around the same corner. All he could see was Janie, in the distance, running erratically. The sound of her calling for Pixie was so poignant it touched his heart.

Maybe he'd been wrong to insist she leave without her dog, yet lingering was taking a terrible risk. Now that Tim was no longer alive, their chances of getting clues from him were zero and it was past time to hit the road.

Brad was sure adrenaline and fright were driving Janie's mad dash. Once she was totally spent, which should not take long, he could easily pick her up. All he had to do was wait a few minutes until her strength was exhausted.

And in the meantime? He was going to keep searching for Pixie for Janie's sake. It was evident she was attached to the dog and therefore being unreasonable. He understood that reaction from an academic standpoint, though not from personal experience. Military handlers bonded that way with their trained K-9s so he was familiar with the concept; he simply had never experienced that kind of connection with a pet.

Pulling over near to where Janie was wading through a blanket of variegated ivy that filled low spaces between ornamental bushes, Brad stepped out of the car. He was deciding whether to wait or plunge in after her when he spotted another dark SUV approaching. It wouldn't have attracted his attention if it hadn't been cruising so slowly up and down the rows.

He ducked behind a parked car. Peered out past the hood. Saw Janie straighten. *No!* Of all the foolish things he might have expected her to do, this was the worst. She was stomping through the eight-inch-deep bed of ivy, making a beeline for the suspected vehicle.

Closing the distance surreptitiously, Brad kept his head down. He was close enough to hear what she was saying by the time Janie began pounding on the closed passenger window.

"Open up, you dog thief!"

The window lowered. "You're nuts, lady."

There was a pause as the driver leaned over to say something to the other man.

Janie answered, "Yes, I am," to the unheard question.

Cringing, Brad clenched both fists, wishing her away from the thugs and praying wordlessly for divine help. He saw her glance toward the area where they'd originally parked, then turn back to the window. "You know very well you were in my car. What did you do with my dog?"

The driver waved his hand at her. Brad could see something white, as if he'd wrapped part of it.

Shaking her head, Janie began to back away with her hands partially raised, palms facing the gesturing driver. It looked as if Pixie had bitten the man and as a result he was furious.

"What did you do with her?" Janie screeched. "Where's my dog?"

Low laughter rumbled from the idling SUV. At the same moment, Brad spotted a flash of white beneath one of the other parked cars. *Pixie? Maybe.*

He chanced a shout. "Behind you!"

Janie whirled. Focused on the cars near

his hiding place. As soon as he thought she could see him, he raised his arm and pointed.

With a squeal, Janie bolted. The driver climbed out of the SUV with his companion, who had a phone pressed to his ear and was nodding.

Janie hit her knees next to the car, trying to coax her frightened little dog to come to her.

Brad went on offense instead of waiting for the thugs to make their next move. Keeping low he worked his way closer and closer to Janie, hoping to spirit her away before the situation went from bad to worse.

"They're coming after you," he shouted to her. "Run."

Of course she didn't. Remaining on her knees she continued to cajole the tiny canine.

Brad closed in. His arms slipped around Janie's waist and he pulled her partly to her feet.

She screamed. Pixie exploded from her

hiding place and lunged at him, catching hold of his pant leg at the ankle. While the dog bit hard and shook the fabric, Janie was able to reach her, pull her into her arms and hold her tightly.

One quick glance told Brad he had only a few seconds left. Reasoning with the stubborn woman would be about as effective as trying to reason with the wiggly, snarling dog. Instead, he kept hold of Janie, who clasped Pixie, and then thudded toward their getaway vehicle.

Tendrils of ivy grabbed at the toes of his boots. *Don't trip*, he told himself. *Whatever you do, don't trip.*

A bullet whizzed by his ear. He swerved like a quarterback trying to clear the way for a winning pass. He was the one pumping adrenaline now and it held him in good stead.

There was no time to open the passenger door so he merely tossed Janie and Pixie in ahead of him, sliding her over with his hip as he grappled with the steering wheel.

Then they were moving. Away from danger. Away from the SUV. He whipped the wheel and skidded the corner—and came nose to nose with another black vehicle. It was the mirror image of the one they had just escaped from.

And it was headed straight for them!

Janie curled into a fetal position, cradling her little pet with her whole torso. Pixie didn't object. "Are you okay, baby?" Janie crooned. "Are you okay? I'm so, so sorry. I never meant for you to get hurt."

The dog's tiny pink tongue bathed her cheeks, wiping away salty tears. *Poor, scared little baby.* "This is all my fault," Janie said to Brad. "You told me to leave her with a babysitter and I didn't."

Because he didn't reply, she called his name. "Brad?"

"I'm a little busy right now," he shot back. "Stay down and hang on. This could get rough."

Assuming he meant they were going to travel over uneven ground, Janie started to sit up. A hand gave her shoulder a hard push. "I said, stay down!"

Hunched over Pixie, Janie drew a stuttering, noisy breath, half sigh, half sob. If this wasn't the worst day of her life, it was certainly among the top ten.

Her car swerved so fast Janie would have been thrown to the floorboard if she hadn't already been half there. She braced herself against the door just in time to keep from getting a nasty whack. Seeking purchase with at least one of her feet, she connected with Brad's ribs.

He blew out an audible "oof" but kept driving.

Janie rose on one elbow to peer out the windshield. They were accelerating toward a large, dark vehicle just like the one she'd pounded on at the other side of the hospital. Was it the same one? Another one? Which?

She swiveled to check behind them. "There are *two*?" she asked in a high-pitched screech.

"At least," Brad shouted over the sound of the racing engine.

Janie suspected he'd stopped himself from expressing a colorful opinion. She understood completely. Sometimes there were no acceptable words for a situation. Like now.

If she got out of this—*when* she got out of this—she was going to enroll in a defensive driving class for sure. Had she been the one behind the wheel, they'd already have been smashed like a bug.

Her car skidded sideways for a moment before the tires grabbed the pavement again. They leaped forward. Brad's knuckles were white against the steering wheel. His jaw muscles clenched.

Janie wanted to praise him. To encourage him. To confess how much she admired his skill and tenacity. If he hadn't come after her and scooped her up the way he did, she could very easily be a prisoner of their pursuers by now. Or worse. She could have suffered the same fate as Tim.

Tears filled her eyes and spilled out.

Pixie licked them away. Brad might be very different than her in the way he handled sticky situations but that didn't mean he wasn't amazing. Whether she agreed with his methods or not, he was still the most awesome personification of a real hero that she'd ever met.

He might not wear a cape and fly through the air or throw thunderbolts at his enemies, but he was more than good enough to suit her. Particularly since he'd stayed to look for Pixie instead of driving away.

Yes, it had occurred to her that the dog might not have been his main reason, yet he had stuck around and pulled her from the proverbial fire once again. Was he hiding a softer side? She certainly hoped so because that was what her father and her brothers had lacked. True empathy was what made people human despite terrible circumstances.

And right now, as Brad was fighting so hard to help them escape, Janie had to admit she was feeling more than mere empathy. She was already fond of the undercover cop. Fond enough that she knew she'd be willing to do almost anything to safeguard his life the way he had hers.

Was it irrational? Yes. Could she do anything about it? Did she want to?

It took her aback to realize the answer was, *No*.

Tires slid. Metal crashed. Janie was jerked back to the present. Had they run into something? The good news was they were still moving.

"What just happened?"

"Our friends met each other head-on at a blind corner. I think they're both out of commission."

"Are you going to go check?"

"Not on your life," Brad replied quickly. "We have a rendezvous to keep, remember?"

"You're not still planning to face these guys to give the drugs back, are you?"

"Do you have a better plan?"

"You know what I think we should do. Go to the police."

"Not yet. I think I can salvage this. I'll tell them you had stolen the drugs and hidden them and I had to partner with you in order to get you to tell me where they were."

"Lovely. Now I'm the bad guy?"

"You won't be anywhere near the exchange point," Brad argued. "As soon as we swap vehicles you'll be free to go."

"How? In my wrecked car?"

"I'll have an officer pick you up?"

"I thought you didn't trust any of them."

"Chief Winterhaven will know who to send. I'll leave it up to him."

"That's not very comforting," Janie replied dryly. "I'd rather stick with you. But not if you tell everybody I stole your drugs."

"Okay, okay, I'll come up with some other reason."

"It's too bad Pixie bit one of them before they could search the car and take this bag off our hands."

She saw Brad's eyebrow arch. "Is that

what happened? I wondered why they'd missed them."

"That's what the guy with the bandaged hand told me. He's apparently terrified of catching rabies and bolted when my brave little dog bit him."

"How did she get out of your car?"

Janie set her jaw, her lips pressed into a thin line, before she said, "He threw her. Can you imagine? The other guy was laughing but the one who was bitten didn't think it was funny."

"I'm sorry," Brad said.

"I think you really are. I thought you didn't like Pixie."

"She's obviously important to you so she matters to me."

Janie bit back tears as she studied Brad's profile. Was this a hint of the gentleness she'd been looking for in him?

She slowly, thoughtfully, shook her head. It was too tenuous to mark a beginning. How many more close calls would they have to have before she met the sensitive man behind Brad's facade of a strong, self-assured, stoic lawman?

Shivering, Janie drew Pixie into her embrace and held her close. It was no surprise that she trusted canines more than she did people. They were honest about their feelings. Dogs didn't pretend to like you. They either did or they didn't, although if they had been abused in the past it was sometimes difficult to gain their complete trust.

The comparison between her own life and that poignant conclusion was patently clear. Even though she wanted to put her trust in Brad the cop, she wasn't so sure about the Brad who ran with criminals.

EIGHT

Brad was thankful he'd opted to stay close to Springfield instead of taking to the Missouri highways because he knew his way around this moderately large city. Oh, it was nothing like KC or St. Louis, but it would do, particularly since he'd once again eluded their pursuers.

He cast a sidelong glance at Janie. She was still cuddling her little white dog and it had fallen asleep with its head resting on her shoulder. The image stirred him in a way he hadn't imagined. No wonder she'd insisted they not leave the hospital parking lot without Pixie. Dog and human were obviously closely bonded. That had to be good for Janie, especially knowing her dysfunctional family background.

He stifled a yawn. They had already packed a week's worth of trauma into one very long day and it wasn't over yet. Pixie wasn't the only one who needed a nap. All three of them were overtired and therefore not at peak performance level. Nevertheless, he had one more goal in mind before he kept his appointment by the boat sales yard in the sporting complex.

"How familiar are you with shooting?" he asked Janie, monitoring the GPS on his phone as they cruised the crowded parking lot in search of their replacement truck.

Her eyebrows arched. She stared at him. "Guns?"

"Yeah. I figured that was a better defensive choice than a bow and arrows or a slingshot."

"Was that supposed to be funny?"

He quirked a wry grin. "Yes. Sorry. But the question is valid. Have you ever shot a pistol or rifle?"

"No. And I have no need to learn how."

"I beg to differ." Brad sobered. "There are several training areas in the basement of the main building here." He checked the time on his phone. "We have over an hour to kill before our meeting. As soon as we change vehicles, I want you to come inside with me and practice."

"Why? We don't have a gun."

He noted that she was pulling her little dog even closer, as if its presence was a shield from whatever she didn't want to do. "You're right. And we can't just buy one without waiting a week for a background check. But there are alternatives. Have you ever heard of paintball? It's a game of pretend combat. The guns fire brightly colored balls that break when they hit a target."

"So? Are we going to paint our enemies and hope they die of fashion shame?"

That brought a chuckle. "No. Handling the paintball gun will train your aim and give you confidence, should you ever be in the position to touch a lethal weapon."

"I told you. I don't want to learn. I don't want to hurt anybody, okay?"

"I get that. I really do. So, tell me. Do

you put on latex gloves when you're dealing with an infectious patient?"

"Of course I do."

"Why? Because you want to be sensible about protecting yourself from an outside threat?"

"It's not the same," Janie argued.

"It's exactly the same." Spotting the pickup truck he was searching for, Brad continued past until he found an empty parking space for her car. "Knowing how to safely use a gun will give you a sense of being in control, whether you intend to use it or not."

"And if I refuse?"

"You won't. You're too smart for that. Besides, if you should come in contact with a firearm and you don't know how to handle it properly, you'll be as big a menace to everybody as those guys in the black SUVs were to us. Guns aren't toys. And they aren't as easy to use as they look in the movies, okay?"

Letting her get out by herself, Brad pulled the canvas dog carrier from the floor in the rear. "Do you have a purse? You're going to need ID."

"I keep my license and a credit card in the case with my phone," Janie answered. "It's in my pocket."

Cupping her elbow, Brad hurried her along. "Okay. We'll move our new wheels across the lot, just in case somebody notices your car and starts to search nearby vehicles. If there's no blanket in the truck I'll toss my jacket over this pink thing so it's not visible from outside."

"I suppose we could leave it with the car," Janie offered.

"What if you need it?"

That brought the ghost of a smile as she said, "I am never letting go of this dog again. Period."

"Okay. Whatever you say. I think if you tuck her inside the front of your windbreaker the store won't make a fuss. I just hope the loud sounds of shooting don't scare her."

"One more good reason to skip my lessons," Janie said.

"Nice try." Brad fished beneath the fender of the waiting white truck and came up with an ignition key in a metal holder. He pushed the button on the electronic key to unlock the doors. "We're good to go. Climb in."

As Janie did so, he took one quick look around. Everything seemed normal. Quiet. Safe.

Unfortunately, thanks to his latest conversation with his chief, Brad knew better. Deadly forces were gathering against him and he was only one person. Unless those dynamics changed, and soon, his chances of success—of survival—were going to diminish even more.

Steeling himself for battle, he slid behind the wheel of the new truck and backed out into the aisle. Chief Winterhaven had promised to have the name of a trustworthy officer of the law placed in the metal key holder box.

When Brad had opened it and looked, however, there had been nothing there but the single key.

* * *

As far as Janie was concerned, Pixie came first. Thankfully, she was so tiny she easily fit inside the zipped front of the windbreaker. Nobody seemed to notice the wiggly bulge as Brad led the way into the bustling shoppers in the sporting goods store. It displayed signs with arrows that pointed to various departments.

"Just like being at the zoo," she commented. "Only here, the animals are *outside* the cages."

"I knew it would be busy. That's one of the reasons I suggested coming here. Anonymity."

"Where's the shooting area?"

"Downstairs." He cupped her elbow. "Stick close. We don't want to get separated."

"If we do, where should I meet you?"

"At the new truck," Brad said. "Don't worry. I won't lose you."

She huffed. "I'd believe that if you hadn't kept trying to get rid of me all afternoon."

"It wasn't personal." He made a face at her. "Okay, maybe it was, a little. I was just trying to do what was best for you."

"Yet we kept getting thrown back together. Doesn't that tell you something?" she asked.

"Yeah. That you're one stubborn woman."

"Well, that, too. I was thinking more along the lines of divine intervention."

"On whose behalf?"

She had to admit he posed an excellent question for which she had no answer at present. That was one of the drawbacks of being human—having a finite mind.

Janie smiled at him. "Has it ever occurred to you that God might be doing a thousand things for us and through us every second of our existence here on earth?"

Brad's resulting expression was so comical and surprised-looking she actually laughed out loud.

He led the way to the indoor gun range, paid the use fees and explained what they wanted to do. He'd have preferred to shoot live ammo in real weapons but given so little time he opted to concentrate on teaching Janie how to use a paintball gun. It was larger than a pistol and smaller than most rifles with a magazine that held the ammo and open sights rather than a scope because the range length was limited.

"Put your jacket over there on that chair," he said quietly aside to her.

"My jacket and…"

"Yeah. Pixie, too, if she'll stay put for you."

"She should. Unless she gets scared."

"These aren't as loud as real guns because they use compressed air instead of gunpowder but you need to remember that they can still do damage, particularly if they're fired up close."

Returning from positioning her dog on a chair beneath the folds of her blue satin jacket, Janie tried to take the gun from him.

Brad held on. "Downrange. Always keep the muzzle pointed downrange at

the targets. Never aim any gun at anything unless you plan to shoot at it." Still,
he hesitated to release the weapon to her.
"I mean it. If you don't learn anything else
today, learn that."

"Got it. Only point at the target."

"Yes. Forgetting that is how even pros
get hurt. All it takes is one moment of
carelessness to affect you and others for
the rest of their lives."

"Have you ever...?"

Although Janie didn't finish her sen-
tence, Brad knew what she was asking.
"I've never accidentally discharged my
weapon," he said solemnly. "But I have
been in a war zone. It wasn't pretty, okay?
I don't talk about it."

"Sorry. I shouldn't have pried. This is
just so serious and scary I was hoping for
some insight."

"You don't want insight," Brad told her.
"If you do have to fire in self-defense, I
just hope you can do it. Hesitation will get
you killed."

Passing her the black plastic paintball

gun he positioned her left hand forward on the vertical grip and her right near the trigger, holding them there with gentle pressure as he stepped in behind her and explained how to look through the open sights.

She shivered. "You cold?" he asked. "You can get your jacket if you need it."

"No. I'm fine. Just a little nervous."

"Okay. Bring the stock to your shoulder, hold it tightly to you, sight the way I told you and when the groove lines up with the front sight gently squeeze the trigger."

To his relief she followed each instruction precisely—until it came time to pull the trigger. Then she gave it a mighty jerk that sent a stream of paintballs arcing toward the ceiling. Brad caught the gun so she wouldn't drop it.

"Whoa! How did I do that?"

He stifled a laugh. "Too eager. Slow down. Be gentle. Ease the trigger back instead of pouncing on it like a cat chasing the dot from a laser pointer."

"Hey!" Janie brightened. "Do these

things come with those? I've seen how they work on TV."

"They do but you don't need one. This is just practical instruction, okay? Bear with me. Let's try again. And this time, slow and easy."

She not only followed his rules, she hit the target dead center. "I did it! Did you see that? I hit it right in the middle!"

"I saw. Good job." He stepped back slowly. "Keep shooting until you run out of ammo. Then we'll reload and move the target farther away."

As soon as she'd emptied the gun she did exactly what Brad had expected her to do. Grinning and proud of herself, she turned to him without laying the weapon aside first.

His fist shot out, grabbed the muzzle and forced it up toward the ceiling as he shouted, "Lesson number one?"

Janie let go, leaving him holding the paintball gun by the wrong end. Her fingers pressed her lips, her eyes wide. "I'm so sorry. I guess I got excited when I did so well."

"Don't let it happen again."

"I won't. I promise."

The visible trembling of her hands, not to mention the way her skin had paled, convinced Brad to halt the lesson. He'd made his point. It was just as well to quit while that dramatic error was foremost in her mind.

He laid the demo gun on the bench in front of them and signaled to the range master. "We'll take one of these—same model, please—goggles, a loader, a box of air cartridges and two thousand balls. Color doesn't matter."

"Yes, sir. Cash or charge?"

"Cash," Brad said. When Janie started to reach into her jeans pocket he stopped her. "This is on me. You keep your money. You may need it later."

Lowering her eyes she smiled. When she looked up, she was actually blushing. "I hate to admit it, but shooting at targets was fun. I'd like to do it again sometime."

"When this is over, maybe we'll play a paintball game for real," he promised. "In the meantime, keep going over what you've learned today so it sticks in your head. Hopefully, some or all of the motions will become natural and you won't have to stop and think every time."

It didn't seem wise to remind her why he'd wanted to teach her to shoot in the first place. Chances were she'd never have to wield a real firearm or defend herself with one, yet it gave him a modicum of peace to know she'd be a fair to good shot if the opportunity did arise. Providing she didn't get too excited or drop the gun when the bang or the recoil startled her, he added to himself.

While Brad paid for their purchases, Janie donned her jacket and scooped up Pixie, tucking her inside once more. He had to admit it made a darling picture with the little white mop of hair, black button nose and dark, shining eyes peeking out where the zipper met in the front. It was good to see some color back in Janie's complexion, too. She wasn't one of those glamour girls who had eyelashes out to here and thick enough makeup to cover any flaws. This woman was a natural beauty with sky blue eyes. He could still imagine the feel of her silky hair when he'd touched it and kissed her outside the hospital.

It would be really nice if I could stop thinking about doing it again, he told himself. Yeah, like that was going to happen. That realization made him wonder if Janie Kirkpatrick had enjoyed their kiss even a tenth as much as he had.

Because the store there didn't sell the cheap cell phones he wanted to buy, Brad quickly led the way back outside, scanning the open areas before heading for their new wheels. "You need to stay with the truck while I make the exchange," he told her.

"You're not going to actually give drugs back to criminals, are you?"

"I have to. This time. It's not ideal, but

if I substituted an inert substance, they'd know I'm not on their side."

"So? After all that's happened, I suspect they're already leery of you."

"You may be right."

"Then you shouldn't do it. It's too dangerous."

Brad shook his head. "Can't be helped. This may be my last chance to ingratiate myself enough to find out who the moneymen are. That's been my goal from the start."

"I know, but..."

He gently touched her arm. "There are some situations that are inherently dangerous yet must be faced. This is one of those. I'm trained for undercover work and you're not. That's why I need you to promise you'll stay out of it."

"I feel so helpless."

That comment brought a smile as he gazed at her walking beside him. "Hey. You have your attack dog and a brand-new nonlethal weapon. What makes you think you're helpless?"

Rolling her eyes at him, Janie also smiled. "Well, when you put it that way."

The truck door unlocked with an electronic click. Brad handed the key to Janie. "Feel free to take your new toy out of the box and practice loading it," he said. "It'll give you something to occupy your time while you wait for me."

There was anxiety in her expression and her eyes glistened when she looked at him. "Only if I can keep an eye on you, too."

"You should be able to see me in the distance. Just keep out of sight so you don't ruin the exchange. Remember, I need to prove myself all over again."

"You've already proved to me that you're crazy-brave," she replied. "I want to go on record. I disapprove of this whole operation."

"Noted." Brad slammed the door and began to back away with the canvas bag in hand. His nerves were probably as taut as hers, and then some, but this was his job. Hers was saving lives in a hospital setting. His was plunging into danger in the hopes of preventing future chaos, future loss of life.

Yeah, he thought. *Starting with not losing my own in the process.*

NINE

Pixie circled half a dozen times before making herself at home in the driver's seat of the unfamiliar pickup truck. Janie had been fingering the plastic bags containing their purchases while she'd watched Brad stride away. He seemed so calm. So in control. So… A lump caught in her throat as her mind completed the thought with, *So dear.*

When had she started to fall for him? she wondered. Visions of the confrontation in the ER popped into her mind. Was it then? Probably, she concluded. After all, he'd not only brought a wounded man to the hospital for necessary care, he'd kept those other thugs from shooting her. She chewed her lower lip. Not to mention deflecting their attack on her car by sacrificing himself and his own vehicle.

Given the usual description of a hero, Brad had it all. "Well, except for the way he seems to fit in so well with these horrible men," she added in a whisper.

Setting sun glared, reflecting off the surrounding vehicles as well as through the windshield. Shading her eyes, Janie peered after Brad, wishing his ordeal was over, yet hoping the criminals wouldn't show up. They would, of course, because he held their drug shipment. It didn't look very imposing, but given all she knew about illegal substances from her work as a nurse, there was plenty in that canvas bag to entice them.

A sudden urge to unwrap and load the paintball gun surprised her. Not one to dismiss intuition lightly she removed the rifle-looking gun and laid it across her lap while she tore at the plastic seals on the packages of ammunition and propellant. Every time she thought she had one almost open, the transparent plastic snapped back and she had to start over. The nail on her index finger broke off so she switched to her thumb.

When she looked up again, she didn't see Brad. Where was he? Moments ago he'd been in plain sight and now he was gone. Her breathing sped along with her pulse. What could have happened to him while she was fighting to open the packaging?

Fisting the key he'd left with her, Janie used it to saw roughly through more plastic and free the box of paintballs. Her hands were shaking and she dropped several before succeeding in filling the hopper to load the gun's magazine.

She grabbed the door handle. Shoved with her right shoulder. "No, Pixie. Stay," was all she said as she dropped to the ground from the high truck cab and slammed the door behind her. There was one sliding window open behind the second seat so she judged her pet to be safe from overheating or escape.

Left hand on the vertical forward grip,

right palming the trigger guard, she crouched next to the truck and began to move toward the area where she had last seen Brad.

Angry male voices reached her before she spotted him. She didn't recognize any of them except one.

"Just hand them over," someone ordered.

Brad's reply was delivered so quietly and calmly she had trouble comprehending. All she managed to hear for sure was, "Here."

"Hands up, away from your belt," a more shrill-sounding voice said.

"Okay, okay," Brad replied. Janie could see him now. His hands were held out to his side but he hadn't raised them all the way. Given the number of passersby, that was probably for the best since he didn't want to attract attention.

Brad had dropped the bag at his feet. "It's all there," he said with a nonchalant shrug that would have fooled her completely if she hadn't known the true situation. The smaller of the two thugs snatched it up and crouched to unzip it while the beefier man kept his hand in his jacket pocket. It was easy to tell he was pointing a gun at Brad through the fabric if you knew what to look for, and Janie did.

What could she do to help? A paintball gun was useless compared to a real firearm. Besides, if she showed herself or gave away her presence in any way it would be bad for Brad. She had to let him work out the deal with those dangerous criminals solo.

Her grip on the paintball weapon tightened. She pressed her side to the nearest larger vehicle, watched and listened.

Oh, Lord, please be with him, she prayed silently, breathing slowly and as quietly as possible for fear anything louder might be overheard.

Traffic continued to inch past as if no one else noticed the confrontation. How long was this going to take? Why didn't Brad just leave? Was he still trying to ingratiate himself with those terrible people?

The larger of the two thugs spoke to his partner, then began to smile.

Brad nodded and stepped closer, offering to shake the man's hand.

That's when Janie spotted the real reason for the criminal's smile. It wasn't because he'd recovered the shipment and was pleased with Brad. That would have been too easy. Too perfect.

Oh, no. He was focused somewhere else.

Janie gasped. Could hardly believe her eyes. What they'd heard transpiring over the phone had apparently been staged for Brad's benefit. Speevey hadn't been eliminated! He was very much alive and sneaking up behind Brad.

She tensed, watching. Her hold on the paintball gun tightened.

Then she saw sunlight reflect off something in the older man's hand. He was brandishing a knife. A big one.

Brad could barely maintain his casual facade. There was something wrong. He sensed it strongly. Intuition wasn't foolproof but he knew better than to ignore the tension in the air or the shiver zinging up his spine and prickling the skin on his forearms.

"So, you happy now?" he asked, addressing his larger foe.

"We will be after we test this stuff," the smaller partner answered for him.

Brad shrugged. "You could take a taste?"

"And let you poison me?" The man's protruding ears were tinged with red as if sunburned.

Managing a chuckle that he thought was convincing, Brad shook his head. "Man, you are too nervous. Did you take lessons from Speevey? Now there's a guy who has no business in our chain of supply, know what I mean?"

"Yeah?" The larger man had taken both hands out of his pocket and folded his arms across his chest. "How come you hooked up with him, then?"

Another shrug lifted Brad's shoulders and he tilted his head as if questioning himself. "I figured any road in was better than nothing. Now that I've proved my-self, I'm ready to play a bigger part."

"What makes you think you'd fit in our organization any better than your old boss did?"

"I'm a lot smarter, to begin with," Brad said, smiling. "And in better shape."

"Not smart enough to stay away from women that'll get you into trouble."

"Hey, that was a big misunderstanding because Speevey wigged out at the hos-pital. I dumped her as soon as I could."

"That's not how it looked to us."

Brad countered with, "She was kinda pretty. Can't blame a guy for lookin'."

The man laughed.

That was when Brad thought he'd won. Had convinced the leader of the team that he was just a regular guy trying to wea-sel his way into a lucrative drug business.

Grinning, Brad started to join in the laughter. He broke eye contact with the first man to look down at Red Ears. Some-thing was definitely off. Not only was he not amused, his ears had colored more, his cheeks were flushed and his eyes had narrowed.

Every muscle in Brad's body tensed. What was going on? What was he missing?

The man's squint refocused over Brad's shoulder. He started to turn and caught movement in his peripheral vision. Something metallic flashed. Well-trained defenses led him to sidestep and duck.

A broad-bladed knife whizzed past his ear, missing by mere inches.

Despite trembling hands, Janie reacted as if she'd just spent a month in a military training program. She whipped the gun to her shoulder, sighted down the long barrel and tried to line up the front and back portions of the sights as she'd been taught.

As soon as the picture looked right she squeezed the trigger. A stream of neon pink–colored balls smacked into Speevey's shoulder.

He let out a yell that was half anger, half surprise, and spun in her direction.

Should she shoot again? Janie wondered. Some of the little balls had ruptured and splashed paint on the side of the evil old man's face while others had hit him and bounced onto the pavement, meaning she was almost too far away, so she inched forward, staying behind parked cars and keeping her head down.

After being hit, Speevey had dropped the knife, his arms cartwheeling as if trying to beat off a swarm of angry bees.

Janie looked to Brad for clues. He'd ducked down and thrown his body to the side, out of the path of the paint, and was now scrambling for the discarded hunting knife.

Red Ears dived for Speevey's weapon, too, while the taller, huskier thug reached back into his pocket and pulled out an automatic weapon. Janie had no idea what caliber it was. It didn't matter. Regardless of what he was carrying, it was bound to be more powerful and far more accurate than her glorified toy.

Given no choice, however, she knew she

had to deflect the man's attention before he shot Brad with real bullets. She rested her elbows on the hood of a handy sedan, bent at the waist to lower her head and shoulders, and took aim again. This time, her target was the lethal weapon the thug was bringing to bear on Brad.

In her mind she could hear Brad coaching her. *Breathe. Concentrate. Then let out your breath and gently pull the trigger.*

Mere moments passed while she fought intense anxiety and struggled to regain control of her quaking body. This was no time to give in to fear. Brad needed her more than ever.

She steadied. Exhaled. Drew a bead on the man with the real gun. And pulled the trigger.

Her stealthy approach had helped both her aim and the effectiveness of the paint-ball ammo. This time its arc was diminished and the balls found their mark with more accuracy. Pink paint splashed on the gun and its user's body, marking both beyond any doubt.

Janie could have cheered. Making a fist she raised her arm and pumped it in the air. "Got him!"

Unfortunately, her victory celebration was premature. Instead of turning the pistol toward her the way she'd expected, the thug shook it, flinging gobs of color all over his partner and Speevey, then wiped it against his jeans. Janie was astonished when he brought it to bear on Brad a second time as if nothing was going to deter him.

By this time Janie was done feeling superior. She concentrated on her aim, sighted higher and set up to fire directly at the man's head.

Everything seemed to be happening at once. Speevey shouted. Brad reached the knife first and leaped to his feet, parrying with the wiry attacker before ducking behind the disoriented old man. The thug fired. Speevey took the first bullet, temporarily sparing Brad.

Janie couldn't believe how still the armed man stood while she steadied her aim. As she squeezed the trigger and held it, only one additional thought raced through her mind. "God, help me."

The line of balls seemed to be traveling in slow motion. The first one hit the attacker in the neck, those following rising fractions of an inch at a time. The final projectile hit his ear, finally breaking his concentration on Brad.

He screamed, dropped the gun and clapped his hand over his injured ear. Feet stamping and howling in pain, he looked a lot less imposing than before.

Fortunately, Janie quickly realized Brad was heading her way at a run. He'd scooped up the paint-covered pistol in passing and was zigzagging between cars and trucks in the nearly full parking lot.

She lowered the paintball gun and spun around. Their truck was close by. And that was clearly where the undercover cop was headed. Giving ground so he could pass her, Janie raced after him, glad she hadn't locked the pickup when she'd left it.

Skidding around the tailgate, Brad raised his hands and yelled, "Keys!"

It took Janie a couple of seconds to remember he'd left the vehicle's key with her. Fishing in her pocket she located it and gave it a toss. A feeble, poorly aimed toss.

Brad had to strain to catch it. "I'm glad you shoot better than you pitch," he said loudly. "Get in!"

Janie was so elated yet still so tense she had to respond in kind. "It was good enough to keep you alive."

Yanking open the passenger door, she shoved the paintball gun and other supplies aside and slid onto the seat in time to hear him answer, "We're not in the clear yet. Hang on."

TEN

To Brad's relief a truck similar to theirs paused in the aisle, apparently wanting their parking place. Anything that would confuse their pursuers, for even a minute, suited him. He'd disarmed the most dangerous of the three men so he felt relatively certain the new arrivals wouldn't be accidentally harmed.

Beside him, Janie was struggling to fasten her seat belt while her little dog expressed his concern behind them. In the closed cab of the pickup, Pixie's high-pitched yips were enough to burst eardrums. Speaking of which…

He accelerated backward, then shifted into Drive and was speeding down the aisle before he said, "That was smart."

"What was?"

"Shooting him in the ear. How did you know that would stop him?"

When Janie didn't answer, he glanced over at her. Everything about her showed that she'd been in a pitched battle, from her flushed cheeks and panting to her messy hair, but it was the expression on her face that provided details.

Brad laughed aloud, triggering the little dog to bark even more. "So, what were you aiming for?"

"Anything and everything," Janie said. She scooped up Pixie, keeping her quiet and away from the wet paint. "His ear just happened to get hit."

"Well, whatever the reason, it worked." He wiped his hands on his jeans, leaving pink streaks. "And made an awful mess."

"Hey, you were the one who said the paint color didn't matter."

"True. At this point it doesn't. See if there are napkins or something in the console to wipe the gun with. We'll stop somewhere and get cleaning supplies so the truck won't be ruined when this stuff dries."

She handed him a fistful of tissues. "Here."

"Thanks. Better than nothing."

"Your clothes are toast, you know. I hope you have others."

"As long as you stay clean, you can shop for me."

"Where? We don't dare stop in town, do we? I mean, what if there are other people looking for us? Now that you're not one of the bad guys, we'll need to convince the good guys we're on their side, right?"

Brad nodded soberly. "Yeah. And then some. As soon as I'm sure we're in the clear I'll find us a place where we can stay to regroup and make new plans."

"New plans? You've been outed. You must have been or they wouldn't have tried to eliminate you just now."

"You're right. We do have one other option. Chief Winterhaven didn't want to use it unless my infiltration failed." He made a face. "Obviously it did, so he's likely to go to plan B."

"Plan B? Does that include me?"

"I hope not," Brad told her. "I don't want you more involved than you already are."

It surprised him when he heard her chuckle so he added, "I mean it. This is too dangerous for civilians."

He saw her eyebrows arch. "What's more dangerous than being shot at and chased around town?"

"Being hit," he said gruffly. "Look, Janie, I know none of this is your fault but there's nothing I can do about it. I think your best option is to change your appearance and leave town until we get a handle on this mess."

"And that will happen when?"

Frustration made him bang a fist against the steering wheel. "I don't know. Nobody does. All I can tell you is that things are coming to a head. With Speevey and his boys out of the way and new men brought in, the operation is on shaky ground. It's my job to see that it stays that way."

"Okay. How are you going to do that?"

His sidelong glance lingered on her as he said, "I have no idea."

The discount store Brad chose for their shopping was far enough from Springfield proper to please Janie. She'd been making a mental list so she was ready when he stopped.

"See if they sell those pay-as-you-go cell phones. And add a couple gallons of water to whatever you get so we can park along a side road somewhere and do a lot of the preliminary cleaning in private."

Janie nodded and got out, speaking through the lowered side window. "Keep your eye on Pixie this time."

"Gotcha." Brad smiled. "If she bites me again, I'll just let her hang on to my finger instead of using a leash."

Janie rolled her eyes. "Great." How that man could go from lethal combatant to comic in the blink of an eye was confounding. Apparently, he was a lot better at compartmentalizing than she was.

When she was scared out of her wits, she tended to stay that way.

"Which is not a bad thing," Janie told herself, entering the country store and smiling at the elderly female clerk who was stocking a nearby shelf with canned goods. "Good evening."

"Evenin'. Grab you a buggy and go to it. Don't dally. I close in a few minutes."

"Okay. Thanks. I'll make it fast," Janie promised.

Beginning in the cleaning aisle, she began to quickly load the cart. Prices were higher but she wasn't about to quibble. The most important thing was getting everything they needed in one stop.

On her way to the dry goods side of the building she picked up a few snacks and a military surplus first-aid kit in spite of the fact that Brad hadn't asked for it, silently praying they wouldn't need it.

There wasn't much choice of denim for Brad but she found jeans in the size he'd given her and added them to the cart, along with a pair of surplus camo pants and a couple of T-shirts in the same blotchy brown-and-green pattern because that was her only option.

A smile twitched at the corners of her mouth as she imagined Brad teasing about her choices. She could almost hear him saying, *That's wonderful for when I'm in the jungles of Missouri*, then laughing.

She knew she'd laugh with him. His good humor was contagious, lifting her dour mood more than once lately. She yawned, realizing how truly weary she was, glanced at the cart and decided she had enough of the necessities. Besides, someone, probably the clerk, was slowly turning off the banks of lights hung from the ceiling.

Rounding a corner, Janie saw a display of foaming cleaner and grabbed a spray can as an afterthought. She set it in the cart near the push handle and continued toward the only checkout register.

There was nobody around. Not the clerk, not a different cashier, nobody. That was odd since they had to know she was still in the store.

A tingle of warning shot up her spine and tickled the hair at the nape of Janie's neck. She shivered. Looked around. The absolute quiet was frightening.

She called out, "Hello! I'm ready to check out."

No one answered.

"Hello?"

Because she'd been keeping a running tally in her head, she knew approximately how much her purchases would cost. Adding plenty for sales tax, she fished a wad of cash out of her pocket and counted off enough to cover the bill and then some.

She had laid the money on the front of the cash register and was stuffing merchandise into plastic bags when she heard a low voice behind her say, "Back away. Hands in the air."

"I wasn't stealing," Janie declared. "I left the money. See? It's right there. In plain sight." She turned with the plastic bag handles looped over one arm. All that remained unpackaged was a gallon jug of laundry soap she'd intended to use to try to clean Brad's clothing.

Her eyes widened. The person who had ordered her to raise her hands didn't look as if he worked there. On the contrary, he was dressed all in black and pointing a flat-sided gun at her that closely resembled the one she'd painted pink earlier.

Scowling, he gestured with the pistol barrel. "Get going."

"Where to?"

"Out the back. We wouldn't want your friend in the truck to interfere, would we?"

"You didn't hurt that old lady, did you?"

A wry chuckle echoed in the silence. "No need. She went into the supply closet without a whimper."

Janie exhaled in relief and purposely picked up the detergent jug by its handle. "Oh, thank God."

"God had nothing to do with it," the armed man said cynically. "I just didn't feel like killing her." He sneered. "You, on the other hand, would be a pleasure."

At least she knew exactly where she stood. If she permitted this man to take her, chances of survival were slim. If she resisted, she might be shot sooner, but given the chances of escape when Brad was right outside versus taking on an armed criminal alone, she figured she might as well give escape a try.

He was looming behind her. Quite a bit taller than she was. She had her hands full at present, which could prove a handicap unless she could use the merchandise as a weapon. Plastic bags would move more slowly than the heavy detergent container so that was the most sensible choice.

Timing was going to be everything, as it was with martial arts. Dropping her purchases would slow her down more than simply swinging the heaviest item so she tensed, readying every nerve and muscle.

It was now or never.

Brad noticed the lights in the store dimming. He didn't like that one bit. Where was Janie? What was taking her so long?

He checked the time. She'd only been gone ten minutes, yet it felt like an hour. If she didn't show up soon he was going to have to venture out despite the pink paint on his clothing and hands.

Pixie had been watching through the windows the same as he had so Brad had rolled the side ones partway up to keep her from jumping down to chase her mistress. The little mutt hadn't seemed to mind the separation at first. Now, she was starting to jump at the door and bark.

That was enough for Brad. The dog might be hyper but she was also sensitive about Janie. Since Pixie thought help was needed, he'd listen to her.

Hand out to keep the dog in the truck, he climbed out, tucking the partially cleaned gun in his waistband at the small of his back and hoping he'd managed to clean it well enough to enable firing. He figured he'd get the first shot out, even if the slide hung up trying to eject the spent bullet casing.

Instead of approaching the glass door of

the store head-on, he went to the wall beside it and edged sideways until he could
lean over and peer in.

At first, he didn't see anything in the
dim interior. Then he looked closer. Every
muscle tightened as he drew the gun.

Janie dropped into a crouch as she spun
and brought the jug up in front of her.
She'd had to guess at how close the thug
was standing when she'd swung from
below and thankfully she had hit him just
where she'd planned. Hard. Effectively.

He'd doubled up and dropped like a
rock, clutching himself and redirecting
the muzzle of his gun toward the floor.

Already primed for her next move,
Janie swung the jug around in an arc and
whacked the back of his neck. The plastic
split like a ripe watermelon. Thick, slippery, soapy fluid ran over his head and
shoulders.

She dodged past him. The race to the
exit was all that stood between her and
Brad. And life.

Unbridled fury behind her almost caused her to falter. A shadow appeared on the outside of the glass door. Oh, no! She was trapped!

If she hadn't been moving so fast and the soles of her shoes hadn't been slippery with soap, she could have changed direction. Instead, she started to slide sideways.

The door opened. Strong arms reached for her. Caught her.

Janie screeched and began to fight.

"Stop! It's me!"

"Brad!" She faltered for only an instant before recovering. "Run!"

Brad released her and shoved her behind him. "Go!"

Janie started to follow his orders until she saw what was happening. Brad had grabbed the handle of the door, pinning one arm of her assailant between it and the jamb. The gun was outside in the man's hand, the rest of him still in the building, while he struggled to free himself.

If that thug managed to lift the gun or

turn it slightly he was going to be able to shoot Brad without ever leaving the store!

Oh, no, he wasn't. She dropped the plastic bags on the ground and reached into the closest one. The white top on the can of foaming cleanser slipped out of her grip so she banged it against the asphalt to jar it loose.

Finger on the spray nozzle, she dashed back to Brad just as he lost his hold on the door and was thrown out of the way.

Janie attacked. The foam reached out. The thug screamed, dropped his weapon and covered his stinging eyes with both hands. She didn't let up until Brad clasped her shoulders and drew her away.

"You got him. And I have his gun," Brad shouted. "Let's go!"

Janie allowed him to practically toss her into the truck. By the time he'd heaved the bags into the back and slid behind the wheel she'd recovered her wits enough to say, "I forgot the water," and heard her partner laugh as if she'd just told him the funniest joke he'd ever heard.

Now, if she could just stop shaking and keep from throwing up, she figured she'd feel pretty good.

ELEVEN

Miles of back roads and highways were behind them before Brad was willing to pull over. It had become obvious that they needed more disguise than a simple substitution of vehicles. He had relayed the information about the attack at the rural store and learned more about what had happened there. Janie's attacker had escaped by the time the sheriff arrived but at least they'd heard that the clerk had been released unharmed.

Sneaking a peek as he drove, Brad noticed Janie rubbing her arms. "Did he hurt you?"

"Not enough to stop me," she replied, sounding actually proud. "I got him good with that gallon of laundry soap before the container broke."

"It was helpful as slime, too," Brad told her. "Well done."

"Thanks. I didn't expect it to spill but that worked out to our advantage, didn't it?"

"Sure did." Hoping his voice didn't sound too tense, he managed a smile. "It's getting pretty late. We need to find a place to sleep and regroup."

"Separate rooms," Janie piped up.

Brad was amused. "Don't you trust me yet? I thought we'd gotten past the stage where you act as though I'm the same kind of guy as your brothers."

"It's not that," she assured him. "It's a matter of propriety. You don't know me well enough to be positive of my personal morals and I didn't want any misunderstanding."

"Fair enough. I'll book us two rooms so you won't be tempted to take advantage of me."

She gave him a playful whack on the arm. "Not funny."

Laughing lightly, he disagreed. "It is to me. You should have seen the look on your face. Priceless."

"Yeah, well, since we're clear about the details, you have my permission to book adjoining rooms as long as the connecting door locks. Never know when I might need to be rescued again."

"Yeah. I'm sorry for sending you into the store alone. I didn't dream they'd still be on our tail. There was no sign of them until that guy pulled a gun on you. He must have sneaked in by the back door."

"I wish he hadn't escaped."

"So do I." Brad's jaw clenched with apprehension. "I also wish we knew how many are after us and who they are. It's hard to dodge an enemy when you don't know what he looks like."

"Ya think?" She rolled her eyes.

"Yeah. I think," Brad said, giving her a lopsided smile. "We're spending too much time on defense when we should be working out plans for a better offense."

"And how do you propose to do that?"

"With help from my chief," he replied. "Winterhaven has connections in and around Springfield. I know he was reluctant to use his old friends before this but I suspect he'll change his mind once I fill him in on what's been happening to us. To you."

"Okay. As long as I don't get into trouble. I can't imagine he'll be thrilled to learn what we've been up to."

"Neither of us is guilty of anything except trying to stay alive," Brad argued. "But first things first. I have to find us a quiet place to hide out."

Janie pulled out the cell phone wallet and turned on her phone. "I'll check. There must be someplace close."

"Turn that off!" Brad was yelling.

Instead of complying, Janie froze and stared at him. "It was off. I just thought I'd use the search app and—"

"And let them locate us again by track-

ing your smartphone," he explained.
"Shut. It. Off."

"Okay, okay. Why didn't you say so in
the first place?"

"I did. I told you to turn it off as long as
we were together and to look for untrace-
able phones to buy in that store. I take it
you didn't find any."

"No. Sorry. They didn't carry electronics."

"Okay. I'm sorry, too. Look, it's possible that truck stops will have what we
need. I'm going to get back on 44 and take
a look."

"What do you want me to do?" Janie
asked, sounding weary.

"Close your eyes and rest," Brad told
her. "I've got this."

That was true. He did have control, he
reasoned, except for the question of his
own cell phone, the one Speevey had
given him. It didn't look like ones that
had a GPS chip imbedded but he could
no longer take the chance it might. As the
truck crossed a narrow, rural bridge over a

running creek, he rolled down his window and gave the little black flip phone a toss.

Janie took note, of course. "You couldn't just turn it off, like mine?"

"Maybe I could have but this way I'm positive it's no danger. We'll replace it—and yours—soon."

"What about the numbers in its memory? Don't you need them to call your chief or report what the drug dealers are using to communicate?"

"I've already relayed their numbers, although I doubt they're still using the same ones. Before you take your nap, how about opening your cell and removing the battery and the SIM card. That will render it totally safe and keep you from turning it back on."

"Do you think I'd forget after the way you yelled at me?" she said with a wry grin. "Not likely. I'm a fast learner."

"I truly am sorry you got involved in all this," Brad said soberly. "If I'd had any idea how bringing Tim to the hospital would snowball, I'd have found another way to get him help."

"Such as?"

Brad shrugged. "Beats me. I just couldn't let him die without trying to save him."

"That's what I love—" Janie stuttered, "*l-like* about you. There's a kind heart hidden under that gruff-looking exterior."

He hadn't missed her slip of the tongue, nor did he blame her. The word *love* had popped into his mind more than once in regard to her. That was terrible, of course. Dangerous. Risky. Tender feelings for his partners were prone to cause trouble, whether the people involved were in law enforcement, like him, or civilians, like Janie.

Drawing his fingertips over his jaw, he kept his glance averted. "I intend to clean up and shave tonight. I don't think I'm going to be pretending to be a street thug for much longer."

"Wonderful," she said, laying her head back and sighing.

Brad decided to keep the rest of his conclusion to himself for the time being. Chief Winterhaven's contacts in the private sector were nothing like the men he'd been dealing with. Nothing at all. They were wealthy, belonged to country clubs and traveled in totally different social circles. Their cooperation wasn't a worry but their well-being might be at stake, particularly if the plan the chief had outlined failed to work.

Therefore, it was going to be up to Brad and a few trusted family bodyguards to keep the participants safe, at least until he had identified and seen to the arrest of some of their acquaintances. That was the tricky part, and why Winterhaven had postponed asking for their assistance.

He sneaked a glance at Janie. Her eyes were closed, her head lolling to the side and resting against the window. What was he going to do with her? Should he keep her with him? Was that even plausible? Yes, she'd been an asset so far but he was about to enter a different world, a world where fitting in was as crucial as it had been to fool Speevey. Maybe more so, since the reach of a nefarious wealthy man far exceeded that of a common crook.

First, he'd run the idea of including Janie past his chief, Brad decided, wondering whether he hoped it would be approved or denied. Then it would be time to see what his volunteer partner thought of pretending to be a socialite.

She was game. He'd give her that. And intelligent, as well. Very few people thought so fast on their feet. When she'd broken away from the would-be kidnapper in the deserted grocery store he'd been both appalled at her bravado and astounded by her quick thinking. Even he might not have thought of using the items at hand as weapons but Janie had handled herself like a fierce commando.

However, when he tried to picture her standing in a crowd, wearing an evening gown and delicately sipping a flute of champagne, he failed. If she couldn't pull it off, or decided not to even try, he'd have to leave her behind. Like it or not, keeping her by his side was only going to be advantageous if she was a better actress than he thought she was.

His prayer, silent but heartfelt, was for more insight.

And maybe a little less running from danger, Brad added. He sighed, then closed by mentioning Jesus and relying on the faith he so often forgot to employ until he was figuratively wading knee-deep in a swamp filled with hungry alligators.

The budget motel next to a busy highway truck stop failed to impress Janie, but by the time Brad pulled into the lot she was ready to sleep right where she sat. Matter of fact, she'd been napping while he drove.

"Good morning," Brad said, smiling.

Janie yawned as she stretched. "Um... morning. It got dark while I was resting my eyes. Where are we?"

"Somewhere between here and there,"

he quipped. "I was starting to get sleepy, too, and figured it was time to stop. This is the best I could find. Will it be okay?"

She nodded as she checked their surroundings. "As long as we got away. You haven't seen any indication we were followed, have you?"

"Nope. Nothing recently." He laid one of their captured guns on the console between them. "Keep this handy while I go check in. Then I'll get you settled and run over to the trucker's store and pick up a few things."

She heard her stomach rumble, and from the amusement on Brad's face, he'd heard it, too. "Like maybe supper?" she suggested.

"And something for Pixie? What does she like on her pizza?"

Janie rolled her eyes. "Make it a plain hot dog or hamburger, if you can. She'd eat the pizza but it's awfully spicy for a little dog."

Brad paused outside the truck and spoke through the open side window. "I'm going to ask for rooms on the back side so we won't be seen."

Smiling at him, Janie nodded. Maybe it was because night had fallen, maybe because she was so weary and maybe simply a mellowing of her heart, but she found Brad particularly appealing right then. He seemed different, somehow, as if getting out of Springfield had changed him for the better.

Perhaps she was different, too, she reasoned, watching him stride away and enter the motel lobby. A few days ago she'd never have dreamed she'd be on the run with a handsome, enigmatic undercover cop and about to check into a low-end motel with him. That notion widened her smile. It was more than just that. A lot more. She was actually happy to be there, to be in Brad's company and to be relying on him as he had come to rely on her, no matter where they were.

Her upbringing had not provided many chances to feel a part of something good, a member of a close-knit group or family that accepted her just as she was, flaws and all. Church had given her a sort of temporary respite. Nursing had come close to providing that kind of daily belonging; at least, she'd thought so until she'd run away with Brad and experienced the fulfillment of her fondest wishes by being around him.

Somebody besides her dog needed her, really needed her, and she was the only one able to give him the emotional and physical support he had to have at present. That notion was both comforting and terrifying. Their tenuous relationship was built on little more than expediency, yet it was as close to perfect as any she had ever had.

To let herself relax and enjoy what was currently taking place. To anticipate the future was absurd. They had to stay alert, above all. Ready for anything.

"And together," Janie added quietly.

Pixie perked up and barked, leading Janie to lean over the seat and release her from the carrier. "The three of us," she added, speaking to the little dog.

Janie was ready when Brad returned with two key cards and handed one to her. She took it without question.

"I got the back rooms I wanted," he said. "I'll drive around and park, then get you settled before I go shopping."

"Should I take the paintball gun with me?" Janie figured the answer would be no but asked, anyway, while her nerves danced the tango in her stomach and her pounding pulse kept the beat.

"Not this time. We have two guns, thanks to our attackers. I'll leave the good one with you. As soon as I get the last of the paint cleaned off the first one, it'll work fine, too."

Janie had to bite her lip to keep from insisting she didn't want anything to do with a real weapon. Instead, she prayed silently that she'd never have to touch it, let alone fire at a human being.

Still, in the depths of her subconscious, an uncomfortable truth lurked. If a loved one was in danger, she would instantly re-think her choices. She'd have to. No way was she going to stand by and let some low-life criminal hurt Brad. Not when she had the power to stop it.

Not even if acting on his behalf went against every life principle she valued? Janie asked herself.

No, not even then. She sighed and accepted her commitment to him, then looked around as if expecting their enemies to be waiting in ambush. As her free hand lowered to rest atop the pistol where it lay, she knew the answer.

She would stand up to anybody and any situation for Brad's sake. And she knew he would do the same for her.

TWELVE

Rain was threatening again. Brad judged he'd have enough time to run over to the convenience store at the truck stop before the storm arrived. He hated to leave Janie for even a few minutes. Logic told him she'd be safer sequestered in the joined rooms with her erstwhile watch dog than going with him so he pulled himself away and jogged over to pick up dinner.

They needed at least two new phones, too, and although he would gladly have bought more he didn't want to attract the clerk's attention. He'd get two now, two or more tomorrow before they left. Being well supplied with cheap instruments they could toss away to keep from being tracked was at the top of his shopping list.

Second was food. Rather than ask for meat without bread and perhaps tip someone to the fact that he was traveling with a dog, he scooped up packaged hot dogs from the warmer tray and a handful of condiments. Add enough mustard and almost anything was palatable. If Janie was as hungry as he was, she'd be delighted with anything he chose.

Two cold half-liter bottles of water completed his order and he piled the food on top of the new cell phones to keep a casual observer from noticing. There were several burly truckers nearby but they didn't seem concerned with anything but themselves and trading anecdotes about highway conditions.

Brad heard them discussing an accident on slick pavement several miles east of there and wondered which direction his chief would tell him to go next. Not that it mattered, as long as he managed to elude the criminals who had been on his trail. *And Janie's*, he added glumly. She was his biggest problem.

Hurrying back to the room with plastic bags from the store, he was about to insert his key card when the door to his room was jerked open. Startled, he asked, "Is everything okay?"

"Yes. No. I don't know," she said, speaking rapidly, breathlessly. "Pixie barked while you were gone so I locked the door between rooms and came over to yours."

"She's probably hungry," Brad offered. He held out one of the sacks. "Here. Go for it."

"I need to walk her first."

"No way."

The little dog was spinning in circles at the closed outer exit and barking. Janie acted worried. "I have to exercise her. It's not fair to make her stay inside and be miserable."

"Then I'll take her." He might have known the stubborn nurse would balk regardless of the risk.

"What if something scares her and she gets away from you? What if she's too shy with you there? What if—"

"Okay. I get the idea. Wait a sec while I grab the good gun." Happily, that brought no argument. Brad slipped the clean automatic into his waistband at the small of his back, pulled his new camo T-shirt over it and peered outside. "All clear. Let's go."

He almost laughed when Pixie leaped through the door before Janie had a chance to open it fully. The little dog hit the end of the leash as if she was pulling a sled in Alaska and didn't let up until she'd tugged Janie to the nearest patch of grass.

Then Brad did chuckle. "You were right. She was desperate."

"Told you so."

"It may surprise you but I never had a dog or any other pets when I was a kid."

"I'm not a bit surprised, considering how little you seem to know about canines. They're really amazing companions. Pixie has been with me since shortly after I got a place of my own. Sometimes I think she can read my mind."

"I wish I could," Brad muttered under his breath. Enormous drops of rain were beginning to mark the pavement like polka dots.

"I heard that." Janie was gathering up her dog and turning toward the motel room.

"You have excellent hearing, too."

Janie smiled. "It's good enough that I can hear your stomach growling. Come on. Let's go eat."

"I hope you like my choices."

"It's food, right?"

Brad nodded. "Yup."

"Then I already love it. We both do, don't we, Pixie?"

Pausing under the eaves, he slipped his key card into the lock and opened the door for her to pass. "After we eat and get cleaned up a little, we'll need to discuss what comes next."

"Why does that sound ominous?"

A tilt of his head accompanied a casual shrug. "Let's just say it's important and leave it at that for now. I have a few calls to make on our new phones before I'll be ready to talk things over with you."

He heard her sigh and noticed the droop of her shoulders. She'd been coping very well, considering. Hopefully, she wouldn't be thrown off by whatever they encountered next.

While Janie fed Pixie little bites, Brad pulled the plastic packaging off his new phones and registered one of them while the other went into his pocket.

Thunder was rumbling outside. Wind-driven rain began to pelt the windows. Dialing Chief Winterhaven, Brad studied Janie and listened to the ringing. She seemed to still have her wits about her. That, or she was very skilled at pretending.

Brad was about to give up when Wes answered, "Yes?"

"It's me, Chief," Brad said. "We had to ditch our other phones so expect me to start checking in from a variety of numbers."

"That's what I figured," the chief said. "How bad is it?"

"Bad," Brad said. He wished he'd called

from the other room so Janie couldn't overhear but it was too late now. "We seem to have ditched our tails for the present but I don't know how long that'll last. Every time I take out one or two guys, several more surface. They're relentless."

"More than you know," Winterhaven replied. "My sources tell me you need to get out of there ASAP."

"Now? Tonight?"

The chief's "Yes" left Brad little choice. Still, he argued. "I think we're safe here for the night and I know we both need the rest. Do you have solid intel about our situation?"

"Unfortunately, I do."

"And?"

"And you should be okay sitting tight for a few more hours. After that, you'll board a private jet at a deserted airfield and it will deliver you to Jefferson City. Once there, you'll be picked up and brought to a friend's house where I'll be waiting and we'll work out our next move."

Brad said, "Hold on," and spoke aside to

Janie. "We have to leave here soon. The chief is flying us to a safe house."

Her jaw dropped. Her face paled. "Fly?"

"Yes. Fly. Do you have a problem with that?"

"Oh, yeah. A big one. I do not fly. Period."

"Well, you'll have to make an exception."

She was backing away, her hands raised, palms facing him. "No exceptions." Janie's gaze flicked past to the window being obscured by pounding rain. "Especially under these conditions."

"Planes take off in the rain all the time."

"Not with me inside, they don't."

Brad put the phone back to his ear. "You heard?"

Winterhaven said, "Yes. This is nonnegotiable. You'll have to leave her behind if she won't come with you."

"Wait," Brad said. "I'm going to put you on speaker."

"You sure?"

"Positive. Janie Kirkpatrick and I are

in this together. It wasn't planned, it just happened. If I leave her, her chances of survival are too slim to even calculate."

"Slimmer than if I fly in a storm?" she asked from the side.

Both men answered together, "Yes."

Brad was moved by the unshed tears he saw gathering in her eyes but not enough to contradict his chief. "She'll go with me," he said, taking the phone off speaker. "And tell the pilot we'll be bringing a dog in a travel carrier, too. That's a must."

"Will do," Wes said. "Hang on and I'll give you the GPS coordinates of the airstrip. You'll need to be there before three in the morning and be waiting with your headlights on high beam to illuminate the numbers painted on the runway."

"It's not lit?" Brad asked, hoping Janie didn't make a run for it over these troubling details.

"No. It's abandoned. There's a reason for choosing it. The Springfield/Branson airport is under surveillance. Law officers and TSA report sightings of several suspicious vehicles. As soon as they were approached they fled, but I'm sure they or their cohorts won't give up trying to silence you. It's a full-blown vendetta. There's only one way around it and that's to put the organizers behind bars."

"Which was my assignment in the first place," Brad agreed. "I'm really sorry things got so complicated. I tried to adjust after Tim Speevey was shot but their organization stayed one step ahead of me."

"That's not all your fault," the chief said dryly. "We uncovered a mole in the department up here in Jeff City and another couple of spies working maintenance and motor pool down in Springfield."

"They were passing info?"

"Almost as fast as you were changing your plans."

"So, they weren't tracing us via Janie's cell phone?"

"They very well may have been doing that, too," Wes said. "I'm still getting reports and trying to figure out who did what. And when. In the meantime, I've given out erroneous information as a diversion. That will help some but it won't be long before the only truly secure place for you will be in the air with a private pilot."

"Won't he have to file a flight plan in order to take off at night?"

"Yes, and no," Winterhaven replied. "He'll file for KC or St. Louis, then divert to Jefferson City once he's airborne. Even if somebody does eventually figure out where you went, they'll lag behind us for a change."

Brad got the details of the rendezvous, then ended the call. He forced a smile for Janie's sake. "It's early yet. The chief figures we'll have time to rest for a few hours. I, for one, intend to shower off the pink paint and clean the second gun thoroughly." He gestured at the door between their rooms. "You'd better take advantage of a chance to nap."

"I won't be able to sleep. I know I won't."

Brad scooped up half the food and escorted her to the shared door. "If you won't settle down for your own sake, do it for your dog's. She must be worn out, too."

He saw her eyebrows arch, her eyes roll. "Oh, please. Is that the best you can do?"

"At the moment, yes." He handed her one of the plastic bags from the store. "Here. If you need anything else, give me about twenty minutes, then knock and I'll go get it for you. Promise you won't go out yourself?"

"I promise." Janie nodded, pausing before she shut the door.

"Lock this from your side and throw the dead bolt on your outside door. Okay?"

"Okay." She sighed. "Thanks."

The urge to give her a gentle kiss was so strong Brad's smile froze. He didn't dare act on his feelings, yet he so wanted to encourage her, to build up her confidence the way it had been when they'd first met in the ER.

He pushed the door until it caught, then heard the lock click into place. So much had transpired since that morning it was incredible. Together they had packed a week's worth of trauma into the past twelve to fourteen hours. And there was more to come. A lot more.

She had to agree to stay with him, Brad told himself. She just had to. Because leaving her to the mercies of the kind of men who had been pursuing them was out of the question. These guys weren't the hicks that the Speevey family had been. These were professionals. Ruthless and coldhearted. They wouldn't make the mistake of underestimating Janie again.

Brad shivered. The sooner they got out of town, the better. His conundrum at present was whether to sit tight until it was time to head for the airfield or to leave the motel earlier and take his chances on the highways. Being mobile had repeatedly led to dangerous encounters. Therefore, it made sense to sit tight and wait until it was time to meet the plane—providing they hadn't already been found.

Checking the parking lot through a slit in the blinds, he saw no current threats.

That didn't mean they were absolutely safe, of course, but it beat spotting another black SUV or, worse, a different kind of vehicle driven by the same bunch of criminals.

Brad huffed. Too bad real life wasn't like watching an old Western movie where the good guys wore white hats and the villains wore black. Their current enemies could come at them from any direction driving any kind of car or truck and he wouldn't know it until they got too close.

Not that he intended to give Janie more details than she needed to know and frighten her unnecessarily, he reasoned, immediately regretting that he hadn't told her more already. She was bright. A true asset. On their way to the airfield he was going to fill her in on as much about the gang as he, himself, knew and trust her to handle the truth well.

She was not going to like hearing how high a price was on their heads any more than he was going to like telling her. According to the chief, the contract was not "dead or alive."

It was just plain dead.

THIRTEEN

Packing for the flight was necessarily light. Janie cleaned out the small canvas carrier she had for Pixie and used that as makeshift luggage. Lipstick was a tube of tinted moisturizer and her hairbrush was a comb she'd borrowed from Brad. Having more than those bare essentials would have been nice but she wasn't about to complain or ask him to shop for her. Not now. Food and elements of protection were essential. Luxuries were not.

She unlocked their adjoining door when he knocked. "I'm ready. Is it time?"

"Almost." He had shaved and drew his fingertips down his cheek to meet his thumb at the point of his chin. "What do you think? Better?"

"Very nice," Janie managed, hoping she didn't sound as happy to see him as she was feeling. "Where did you get a razor?"

"At the truck stop. I would have gotten things for you, too, if I'd known what you needed."

Janie smiled as she began to relax a little. There was something comforting about being with Brad, but rather than overanalyze she simply accepted it. "Next time, how about a hairbrush and toothbrush. I'm beginning to feel almost as scruffy as you used to be."

"There are some toiletries in the bathrooms. Didn't you look?"

She humphed. "Look? I laid down on the bed with Pixie and the next thing I remember is hearing you knock on this door."

"Told you you were tired."

"No kidding." Turning, she donned her jacket and picked up the dog carrier. "I put my old clothes in here. There's a little more room if you want to stash yours."

"I'm ditching the shirt and jeans," Brad

said. "They were hopeless. Everything I own at this point I'm wearing."

"Too bad I had to use that laundry detergent as a weapon. It might have gotten your clothes clean."

"It served a better purpose," Brad said, sobering and stepping back. "Come on. And bring Pixie. It's time to make a run for it."

The way he said it gave Janie the shivers. "Run? Did you see any of those guys again?"

"No." Concern shadowed his handsome face and a lock of wavy dark hair swung to rest on his forehead.

Janie studied him. "I sense a 'but' coming. But what else?"

"Nothing certain. When I spoke to the chief privately, he indicated that he'd uncovered spies within his department as well as in the Springfield area. That's why it's so important for us to get to the airfield without being seen."

"What if we are? Can we still go?" It

went without saying that she was hoping she would *not* have to fly.

"We have to," Brad said flatly. "Wes gave out false information about our travel plans, which should help temporarily. As soon as the gang figures out they've been tricked they'll start fanning out and checking likely routes out of town. That's why I didn't want to be traveling any more than absolutely necessary. We'll go straight to the airstrip from here."

"Is it far?"

"No."

Hesitating, she felt him place a hand gently at the small of her back and guide her forward. Pixie was circling and dancing at their feet so Janie passed Brad the carrier and scooped up her little pet. Holding the affectionate dog close seemed to help calm her while errant thoughts of having to board any airplane, particularly a small one, gave her the shakes all the way to her toes.

"I—I don't know if I can do this," Janie admitted. "I mean it. I'd rather face those thugs in their big SUVs than get on a plane." She paused again as Brad opened the outside door. Rain was still falling, although not as heavily as it had been. In the distance she could see flashes of light and hear the rumbles of thunder.

"We'll be fine," he assured her.

Janie's wry wit surfaced as a defense and she said, "I hear that's what General Custer told his troops before Little Bighorn."

Brad quirked a smile. "That's better. I've missed your sarcasm."

"Yeah, well, consider it a last resort. I tend to get silly right before I fall apart completely." She sobered. "It used to get me slapped by my brothers pretty regularly."

Brad didn't comment until he was behind the wheel and pulling out onto the highway. "I was sorry to hear you didn't take advantage of the escape the department offered back then. Why did you stay at home after everything that had happened?"

"They were family. Bad or good, I didn't want to leave them and go live with strangers. I waited until I was old enough to get by on my own."

"You were, what, sixteen?"

"About that. Once I got involved in martial arts training and made some friends through that program, I was able to rely on their support. It actually worked out better because it gave me a skill to fall back on while I studied nursing."

"Good for you."

"Thanks. It wasn't easy but it was worth it."

"So, you got through all that by yourself or with the help of a few friends. Surely, you can bring yourself to trust a skilled pilot as long as I'm with you."

Janie rolled her eyes and held Pixie closer. "Only if you happen to come with your own parachute." His warm laugh sent a shiver of awareness singing up her spine and prickling the tiny fine hairs on her arms. It was probably better to kid around about her fears than to spell them

out. Not that she could. A nameless, face-
less sense of dread was hard to explain,
which was another reason why it was so
hard to banish.

Lightning jumped from cloud to cloud,
illuminating them from within and distracting Janie from her immediate surroundings. The seconds between each
flash and an ensuing boom were impossible to count because the sky was so ac-
tive, so filled with menace. Surely, aircraft
were susceptible to being struck the same
as a tree or structure on the ground. What
then? Did the electronics fail? Was she
going to disappear like those planes that
flew into the Bermuda Triangle?

Janie shook herself, disgusted with the
direction her thoughts had taken. She
sat up straighter. Cuddled Pixie gently.
Glanced in the rearview mirror on her
side of the new truck.

"Brad!" Staring, she was incredulous.
"Look back there!"

She saw him lean to the side, trying to

see what she meant. "It's too dark. What do you think you saw?"

"A couple of big vehicles," Janie said. "Wait for a flash of lightning, then look."

"I still don't..." Suddenly, he accelerated.

Pushed back against the seat, Janie knew she'd been right. Or at least Brad thought so because his speed had greatly increased and he'd begun weaving in and out of what little traffic happened to be on the road before dawn.

She could hardly breathe. Her pulse pounded. Another flash showed vehicles trailing them in that same swerving path.

"How much farther?" Janie shouted over at him.

"Two, maybe three miles." Brad continued to zigzag until he reached an eighteen-wheeler and cut in front of it. The trucker laid on his horn. Brad continued to the right, slipping onto an off-ramp at the last possible second.

Janie was scared to death—and elated. "You did it. You lost them!"

"For a few miles, maybe. If they know where we're going, they might be there waiting for us."

"I didn't need to hear that," she warned, clinging to her sense of victory.

"Yes, you did," Brad countered. "Keep your head down as best you can and hang on. This isn't over yet."

"Do you have any more tidbits of terrible news you'd like to share?"

"Not at the moment."

Watching his masterful driving, Janie was struck by how much safer she felt when he was behind the wheel. Knowing she, herself, was a good driver wasn't enough to provide a sense of relief whereas having Brad in charge was. So much for her feminist mindset, she admitted ruefully. It was one thing to feel powerful and capable in normal situations and quite another for that sense of strength to carry over into this kind of situation.

Two were definitely better than one and having the police officer as the second member of her team was an unfathomable advantage. To have ended up like this was so far-fetched she was forced to attribute it to divine intervention. That, or deny everything that had brought them this far in one piece.

Brad slowed. Turned down a dirt track. The truck's headlights illuminated a chain hanging across the road with a No Trespassing sign swinging in the center.

"Stay here," Brad shouted as he threw open his door and ran toward one of the posts supporting the end of the chain.

Janie held her breath. Pixie barked. Brad hunched against driving wind and raindrops the size of dimes. Lightning revealed the airstrip beyond. Unimaginable fear had reached its peak, or so she thought, until other pairs of lights appeared in the distance behind them.

"Hurry," Janie yelled out the open door. "Somebody's coming!"

The momentary expression on Brad's face was more frightening than anything he could have said.

Racing back to the truck he slid behind

the wheel and hit the gas, letting their forward momentum slam the open door.

"Is it them?" Janie kept trying to see better.

"Almost has to be," he shouted back. "Get ready to pile out and run."

"Do you have the guns?" Janie asked.

"Yes." He released one hand long enough to pull a pistol from his waistband. "Here. Take this."

The slightest hesitation brought his ire. "Do it. Now! You don't have a choice."

She was reaching for the gun when he added, "You might be the only chance I have of living through this."

That was enough. Her fingers closed around the grip, her finger beside the trigger guard as he'd instructed. She rested her thumb on a tiny button. "Is this the safety?"

"Yes!" Brad turned the wheel abruptly and hit the brakes. The rear of the truck slid sideways. Its headlights now lit the gigantic white numbers painted on the asphalt.

Above and to their right, a set of landing lights flicked on while beacons on the wings and tail of the approaching plane continued to flash.

Janie abandoned everything but her dog and the pistol as she left the truck and ran.

One glance told her that Brad had taken up a position behind the open driver's door and was drawing a bead on the road behind, centering on the pairs of headlights.

Forgetting her qualms, Janie positioned herself on the center line of the paved runway and began waving the gun to signal the plane while clasping Pixie in her other arm. Landing gear descended. The engines changed pitch and slowed.

She looked back at Brad. He was standing firm. Defending their position until the last moment.

FOURTEEN

Brad saw the plane land, pivot and taxi back to where Janie was standing. Her hair blew wildly, her jacket flapping in the gale. Sound told him the engines were idling, ready to be pushed for takeoff.

He snatched a brief glance, saw a hatch with steps drop down and someone reach to help Janie on board. In front of him the pairs of headlights parted as one vehicle diverted. He couldn't let them get around him and block the runway.

Aiming slightly behind the lights, he fired a burst where he thought the front tires would be. The targeted vehicle swerved abruptly, then came to rest pointed directly at him.

Someone bailed out and returned fire.

Brad countered. The second set of lights was barreling closer and closer. His pistol ejected the final casing and the slide stayed back. He was out of ammo. It was now or never.

Pivoting, he dropped into a crouch and headed for the plane. To his amazement, flare from the barrel of another pistol illuminated the door at the top of the ramp. Somebody was firing, covering his escape. Was it Janie? Had she actually overcome her loathing of firearms enough to defend him?

Straightening as he took the final leap to the foot of the ramp, Brad saw her. His heart swelled. She had taken up a position in front of the open door and was laying covering fire.

"Get inside," he shouted as he took the steps two at a time. His hand deflected the gun. His open arms scooped her up and they tumbled into the plane together while Pixie did her best to find a place to bite him.

The gangway was still rising as the pilot

gunned the engines. A second man secured the hatch and returned to the cockpit. The aircraft vibrated beneath them, then lifted off at a steep angle as Brad held Janie close.

He knew he should release her but something in him kept refusing to let go. "Are you hurt?" he finally asked.

She was clinging to him. "No. You?"

"I don't think so."

Raising her head from where it had been resting against his chest she peered at him through the gloom of the dimly lit cabin. "You can't tell?"

"Sometimes not," he answered truthfully. "Adrenaline can mask pain for a short time. I didn't feel anything hit me, though."

"Neither did I."

When she pressed her cheek into his shoulder, Brad felt her shudder. He said, "That was a very brave thing you did."

A delicate snort preceded, "And stupid?"

"Not in my opinion. If you hadn't pinned them down, I don't know if I'd have made it."

"Well, I can't take all the credit," Janie admitted. "One of the pilots was shooting, too. He'd stepped back to reload so I took over."

"Whatever. You stood your ground. I'm very proud of you."

Feeling her starting to relax, Brad loosened his hold and got to his feet, reaching out to help her stand while he braced himself on the side of a passenger seat.

Janie never left her knees. "If it's all the same to you, I'd rather not stand up. This thing is tilting and pitching like a rowboat at sea."

"We'll smooth out as soon as we gain a little more altitude."

As soon as he'd helped her into one of the seats, Pixie made a dive for her lap. Brad made sure Janie's safety belt was fastened before he sat next to her. It wasn't a big surprise to feel her try to snuggle closer, dog and all.

Relief washed over as if somebody had poured warm water from his head to his feet. He slipped an arm around her shoulders and drew her even closer. In retrospect, it seemed impossible that they had weathered so many attacks and come through unscathed. Yet they had.

It wasn't over, of course. Not by a long shot. But this was a much-needed respite and he intended to take advantage of it.

Lightning continued to flash outside the small, twin-engine plane. Air turbulence hadn't decreased the way Brad had expected and he sincerely hoped Janie could take the rough ride without experiencing motion sickness. He wanted her to be able to relax. To rest. To recoup enough for their next challenge.

Time passed. Her head stayed against his shoulder and he continued to hold her, relishing every moment. Pixie didn't seem to mind, either. When he reached across and completed the embrace with both arms, she licked his wrist. Including the feisty little mutt wasn't exactly Brad's idea of the perfect hug but he went ahead. At this point, he'd have used any excuse to hold the woman who had become so vitally important in his life.

"Whatever is left of it," he murmured, checking to see if she reacted and finding her nearly asleep. He leaned close enough to place a light kiss on her hair, then her forehead.

His eyes met Pixie's. One side of the little dog's mouth twitched in a half-hearted snarl.

Brad smiled at the dog. "It's okay, girl. You and I can look after her together."

The black button eyes blinked.

"Yeah," Brad whispered. "You can tell how I feel, can't you?"

Another blink. Then a lick of the nose.

Brad barely uttered a sound when he added, "Yeah. I love her, too." Smiling, he added, "It'll be our secret."

Janie had tried to keep her eyes open as they flew but there was something soothing about the vibrations of the aircraft despite its pitching and yawing. It had also felt good to have Brad's arms around her, although if he had asked she would have denied enjoying it so much.

Her mind had drifted, reliving bits and pieces of their prior moments together and marveling at their survival against attacks that should have been overwhelming. Yet here they were.

Sighing, Janie had felt herself falling asleep and quit fighting her drowsiness. There had been times in the past when her dreams had been supersweet but none had come close to the emotions she was experiencing at present. She envisioned herself as a princess in a beautiful ball gown being whirled around a dance floor by a handsome prince. No one else existed. Just the two of them.

The music began to fade. The prince pulled her closer. She felt his warm breath against her forehead just before he kissed her there.

His expression of adoration carried over into reality and Janie smiled, stirring slightly. She sighed just as she heard him mention love and held perfectly still, waiting to hear more.

Brad's cheek was resting against her head, his breath tickling the fine hairs by her temple. She felt his muscles starting to relax, heard his breathing slow and even out. He, too, had surrendered to sleep. The poor man had to be exhausted, she reasoned, determined to stay quiet and let him enjoy what respite he could. He deserved weeks of R and R instead of a few stolen minutes here and there.

Janie lifted her right hand off Pixie and slipped it around Brad's waist above the safety belt. That was the best hug she could manage so she added as much as possible by turning her head slightly and kissing his shoulder.

The leather of his jacket lay between them but Janie didn't care. As far as she was concerned she'd kissed him.

Her fondest prayer, other than survival, of course, was that she would someday have the chance—and the courage—

to show him how she felt when he was awake.

"I can. I will," Janie whispered to herself before realizing they first had to live through their current ordeal. She added, "Lord willing," and asked God for His blessing and ongoing protection.

Without raising his head or giving any other sign he might be awake, Brad pulled her closer. Janie was already sighing softly when she heard him murmur, "Amen."

A sense of peace encompassed Brad as he fought to awaken. The more alert he became, however, the more that feeling faded. Finally, he couldn't stand sitting still and eased his arms from around Janie so he could get up and speak with the pilots. She did stir, as did Pixie, but quickly settled back against the seat with her eyes closed.

Attempting to walk forward he caromed off the bulkhead twice before he was able to put a steadying hand on the back of each pilot's seat and lean between them to ask, "How much farther?"

The copilot on the right replied, "Longer than expected. We've diverted to try to avoid the worst of the storm. As you can see, it's still plenty bad. Sticking to our flight plan and landing in Jefferson City may be tough."

"Unless you want to be met by more gunfire, I recommend we not follow your original flight plan," Brad warned, waiting to see what their reactions would be. The copilot looked confused but the pilot nodded.

"Copy," the pilot said, glancing to his right. "I've been fully briefed."

"That's crazy," the copilot argued. "In these changing winds we'll need all the runway choices we can get."

Brad watched the tense exchange, thankful that at least one of the men at the controls knew what the original plan had been.

The pilot was shaking his head and spoke firmly. "We won't have a problem. This storm has provided the perfect excuse to divert and we will. I have no qualms about landing on our home field." His voice hardened even more. "If you're afraid of a little tricky flying, I suggest you go back and sit with our passengers."

Although the copilot clearly disagreed he stayed in his seat, hands on the controls, jaw muscles working as if he was clenching his teeth.

"Anything more you'd like to share?" the pilot finally asked.

Brad shook his head. "Sorry, no. Just get us on the ground in one piece and we'll take it from there." Observation told him that both pilots were fatigued. Instruments would handle just so much bad weather. Pilots were expected to smooth out the rest of the ride and these two had obviously been working hard to do so.

"Can we expect to fly out of this soon?" Brad asked, hoping the answer was yes.

"That had been the plan. It sure would have helped if you'd picked a nicer night to need us."

"Yeah, well, as you saw, it wasn't up to me." Brad huffed quietly. "Thanks for the timely arrival."

The copilot squared his headset snuggly, concentrated on flying and kept the rest of his opinions to himself. It was the pilot who replied, "From the looks of it, about five minutes earlier would have been even better." He eased away slightly in order to stretch, then offered to shake with Brad. "Captain Jace Madison. Former US Air Force."

"Detective Brad Ross... I mean, Benton." He chuckled. "I've been undercover for so long I forgot who I really was."

"I take it that's over now?"

Brad nodded. "Yeah." A tilt of his head toward Janie preceded, "I kind of blew it when I rescued her."

"Why head north? If I may ask."

"You can ask. Even if I had answers I probably wouldn't tell anybody, no offense meant."

"None taken. My orders were to pick

you up and deliver you. Beyond that, it's up to the folks we work for."

"Who would that be?"

Jace's eyebrows arched. "You don't know?"

"Nope. My police chief arranged everything. He's meeting us when we land."

"Maybe he is. A lot will depend on whether we manage to get this bus down anywhere close to Harold Armbruster's estate. He's the guy picking up the tab."

A flash of lightning outside the front window of the aircraft passed so close its zigzag pattern left an image in Brad's sight for long seconds.

From the floor he saw the pilot whirl and grab the wheel, reaching with his right hand to check instruments. He flicked a finger against several gauges repeatedly.

Brad stayed down but shifted onto his knees. "What happened? Are we okay?"

Neither pilot answered. That figured. They were both really busy at the moment. One quick glance at Janie showed him where he belonged.

Brad crawled back to her, rather than try to stand, and hoisted himself into his seat. Her eyes were wide, her lower lip quivering. She looked terrified.

"It's okay," Brad assured her. "Just lightning."

"It looked like it hit us!"

"Yeah, it was pretty close." He forced a smile. "You should have seen it from the cockpit. Quite a fireworks show."

When he tried to slip his arm around her shoulders again, she leaned away so he backed off.

"What aren't you telling me?" Janie demanded.

"You know everything I do. Honest. These guys are pros. The best thing for us to do is sit back and let them do their jobs."

Before Brad could say more, the captain shouted over his shoulder at them. "Some of the nav instruments are out. We're going to drop down and fly the rest of the way VFR—visual flight rules."

Janie clutched Pixie closer as they both

trembled. There was no need for Brad to tell her how much more dangerous this kind of navigation was, particularly at night in a storm.

It was bad enough that he, himself, knew.

FIFTEEN

Janie had to bite the inside of her cheek to maintain self-control. Every trial she and Brad had faced so far had allowed her to take some defensive action. To think her way through and come up with a solution. This time, there wasn't a thing she could do except sit there and pray for deliverance.

Which wasn't a bad idea, she realized, ashamed of herself. Had she been too self-assured, too proud, to admit she needed God's help to get out of this fix? Probably. No, definitely.

Clasping her hands below her chin so she could still keep hold of Pixie, Janie closed her eyes and began to silently pray.

She felt the warmth of Brad's hand covering hers, peeked out at him and saw that his head was also bowed, his eyes closed, so she gave voice to her plea. "Father, help us. Please."

It wasn't necessary for Brad to speak for her to know he was agreeing because his fingers tightened around hers. That was a bond that gave her heart so much peace and joy she was rendered speechless.

When she finally said, "Amen," she felt Brad kiss the back of her hand. Where fright had failed to loose her tears, his gentle kiss succeeded.

When she raised her gaze to his, moisture was streaking her cheeks.

Cupping her face in his hands, Brad swept the drops aside with his thumbs. "It'll be all right, Janie. I know it will."

All she could do was nod. What she wanted most was to be back in his tender embrace, dreaming sweet dreams, unaware of the danger they were currently facing. What little she knew about flying came from watching movies and television but she was pretty sure flying solely by sight in this kind of weather was terribly risky.

Swallowing, she felt her ears pop as they descended. There was nothing to see out the windows, and from what she could tell, all the pilots were seeing was rain, clouds or fog, and flashes of light. How they expected to identify landmarks on the ground and navigate safely was beyond her.

This time, she didn't resist when Brad put an arm around her shoulders. She did, however, try to lighten her own mood by lightening his. "How are you at math?"

His brow knit. "What?"

"Math. Are you good enough at it to calculate our odds of survival?"

"I take it you're kidding."

She huffed. "Kind of. I'd actually rather be shooting paintballs at some lowlife in a parking lot than hurtling through the air at night guided by iffy instruments."

Brad slowly nodded and Janie could tell their minds were attuned before he said, "Yeah. Me, too. I guess it's a matter of wanting to feel as if I'm in charge." After giving her shoulders a squeeze he added, "You were amazing when you took out Speevey like that."

"All I did was distract him and his buddies so you could fight back."

"I'm sure glad you did. I'm not usually so careless. You saved my bacon."

At the mention of food her stomach growled. Thankful that the noise of the plane drowned it out, Janie realized how hungry she was. "I could use a BLT right about now. With a soda."

"Seriously? You can eat at a time like this?"

Janie gave him a genuine smile. "I'm a woman. Most of us either stop eating under pressure or stuff ourselves. I'm the kind who finds solace in food. I hate to admit it but I'm starving."

Leaning away, Brad unfastened his seat belt. "Hang on. I'll see if there are snacks stowed in the back."

She grabbed his forearm. "No! It's too

dangerous to be up walking around. What if we crash?"

With that, he laughed. "Honey, if we go down in this little plane it won't matter whether I'm strapped in or not. It's gonna leave a mark."

She didn't have to force herself to smile again because, despite their tenuous situation, she was with Brad. For some crazy reason, his presence soothed her nerves and she decided it was best to put off questioning that reaction. Once they had landed and were safe, maybe she'd think it through. And perhaps then her mind would have a plausible answer because right now, right here, she was at a loss.

Keeping Pixie close, Janie consciously slowed her own breathing and fought to maintain an aura of calm until Brad returned. When he did, his arms were full.

"Bottled water, nuts and candy bars. There was nothing in the fridge back there but I found other goodies."

"Thanks." Janie drank almost a full bottle of water before coming up for air and offering Pixie a drink from her cupped hand. "I didn't realize how thirsty I was."

Noticing how Brad was holding back the candy, she laughed. "Don't you share?"

"Candy isn't good for you."

"Tactful, as always. What you were really thinking is how fattening it can be." She held out a hand, palm up. "Give. I've burned off more than enough calories hanging out with you lately."

He gave her a choice before opening one for himself. "As soon as we land, we'll ask my chief to take us to a drive-through burger joint."

Janie waved what was left of her candy bar. "You really know how to show a girl a good time."

"Can't complain you're bored, right?"

"That's a fact."

The plane had leveled out, making it easier to drink, and Janie finished her water. "Were there more of these?"

"Here. Take mine."

She didn't hesitate except to salute him with the bottle. "Thanks."

"Anything for my best buddy."

His casual response sounded slightly affectionate despite the choice of words. At least she imagined it did. Some of her dreams during this flight had been more special than that but she was beginning to doubt they'd had any basis in fact. Nevertheless, it was pleasant to recall bits and pieces of the experience, particularly those in which Brad had shown affection for her.

"How much can you tell me about what to expect when we land?" The question had been more to let him know she trusted their survival than it was to learn details.

"Not a lot," Brad said. "Chief Winterhaven has connections in the capitol and told me he was implementing plans to use us up there."

"Me, too?" Although she was willing to help Brad she wasn't sure she was ready to place all her trust in the unknown the way he was.

"If we can work it out, yes," Brad replied. "How are you at playing a part? You know, acting like a different person."

That made her smile wistfully. "Me? Oh, I don't know. You've watched me go from a sensible nurse to an armed combatant in the space of twenty-four hours. What do you think?"

"Yes, but that's because it was expedient, not a role in a staged drama. The chief indicated he was going to ask me to pretend to be wealthy so I'd fit in. Can you do that?"

"What? Pretend I wasn't raised on the wrong side of the tracks and didn't come from a family that almost killed me? Sure. Piece of cake." Pausing, she took a last sip of water before she added, "I've been doing a pretty good job of convincing you I'm not scared, haven't I?"

He raised an eyebrow at her. "When?"

Janie huffed derisively. "Try all the time. From the moment I flipped that guy in the ER and the gun went off, I've been pretending I have my emotions totally under control."

Brad patted her hand and started to

stand again. "Hang in there. I'll go get us more water."

As he straightened, the plane gave a lurch. Janie made a grab for his hand. Missed. Watched him thrown to the floor.

She screeched, "Brad!"

He was sliding down the aisle toward the cockpit. Janie could see both pilots straining against the controls, apparently trying to halt the dive.

Janie knew she didn't dare unfasten her belt or she'd be in the same boat as Brad. She leaned forward as far as she could with Pixie in her lap. It was no use. She was yards away from being able to reach any part of him, even his shoe.

The slide ended when he connected with the bulkhead. Seconds later, the plane righted. Brad didn't move.

"He's hurt!" Janie shouted.

Neither of the pilots paid any attention to her.

Brad's eyes popped open. His vision was blurred. He put a shaky hand to his temple to see why his head was throbbing and exhaled a weak, "Ow."

A figure was hovering over him. Blinking to clear his sight, he almost gasped. "Janie."

"Easy. I'm checking your neck and spine," she said, all business. "Don't move."

Brad's hand came away slightly bloody but he otherwise felt uninjured. "I'm fine."

"I said, don't move."

He ignored her. "I'm on the inside and I can tell you, the only damage done is to my pride and a little piece of my hard head. Honest."

She rocked back on her heels, giving him the kind of stern look he remembered his mother using when he was being particularly difficult as a boy. She didn't have to say he was acting stupidly to get her point across. Her expression was doing it for her.

He relented. "I'm okay. I promise, Nurse."

"It's not a joke. I'm the trained professional and right now you're my patient. You'd be smart to let me do my job."

"Right." He straightened his bent elbow and eased back down. "Hurry it up. You need to get yourself back into your seat and keep your belt fastened."

"Oh, like you did?"

"I was on a water bottle run," Brad argued. He looked toward the cockpit and raised his voice. "Will you be able to hold us steady for a bit?"

The pilot nodded. "Looks like it. I know where we are. When you hear the gear coming down, we'll be close to landing."

"Thanks." He focused back on Janie. "Okay. Do your stuff if it will make you happy. I'm going to count to a hundred and then get up, regardless."

As she leaned closer, her silky hair brushed his cheek. The thoughts those actions stirred were unwelcome but only because he felt they were wrong, at least for the present. When all this was over, given the way his affection for Janie was growing, he was already trying to figure out how to begin dating her for real.

Rocking back again, she took his closest hand. "Squeeze my fingers."

When he obliged, she added, "Is that the best you can do?"

"I don't want to hurt you."

"I need to check your strength to tell if there was nerve damage. Squeeze."

As soon as he did, she let go and took his opposite hand. "Again. Hard."

All Brad was concerned about was her, yet he managed to do as she'd asked, within reason. "Satisfied?"

"Yes." Janie pushed off, turned and crawled back to her seat where Pixie waited and eagerly slurped her forehead before inching away to make room.

Brad gladly followed. Since the slight injury to his scalp was on the same side as Janie, he allowed her to lift his hair and probe it again. "No stitches. It'll spoil my image," he said.

"If you needed them I'd insist but it looks minor. The face and head are very vascular so they always bleed a lot. You'll live."

"Can I get that in writing?" he teased purposefully.

"Only if you promise to ensure that it remains true."

"I'll do my best." Some of the concern he'd noticed before had left her expression and she once again looked weary. That figured. She was used to excitement working in the ER but nothing like the marathon they'd been put through lately. They both desperately needed sleep and the comfort of a safe house.

She made a grab for his hand as a grinding, whirring sound filled the air.

"That's just the landing gear," Brad told her. Nevertheless, he didn't let go of her slim fingers. On the contrary, he closed his other hand over hers and clasped it firmly.

"You're sure?"

"Positive."

Her sigh was audible. "Thank God. Literally."

"Not a bad idea," Brad said. "And while you're at it, you might mention asking for safe passage after we land."

"Done and done." Closing her eyes, she was breathing so shallowly Brad wondered if she was holding her breath.

"They wouldn't have lowered the gear if they didn't see the airfield," he said, looking out the porthole-size window to his left. "They're lowering the flaps to slow our speed. We're almost there."

"Then you know how good an actor I am," Janie said, turning wide blue eyes on him. "Because inside I'm screaming hysterically."

"Really?"

"Oh, yeah." She nodded. "And then some."

"The acting trophy is yours, then. I'll even have your name engraved on it if you want." Of course his banter was meant to distract her and he didn't doubt that she knew it.

"It had better be gold and ten feet tall,

then, because I will have earned every inch of it by the time we hit the ground."

Brad laughed and patted her hand. "Bad choice of words but I get the idea. Let's plan on rolling down the runway instead of hitting it, okay?"

Just then there was a bump and a squeal that sounded like car tires spinning on wet pavement. The plane pitched forward slightly, then settled and began to slow.

Brad was so relieved, so overjoyed, he dropped his guard for a split second. That was long enough for Janie to lean closer and kiss his cheek unexpectedly.

A wide grin split his face. "Thanks, but I didn't do anything special. The pilots should get all the credit. That was some awesome flying."

"I know." She grinned back at him. "I'll kiss them, too, if you want."

"Never mind. You don't want them to get the wrong idea."

Her smile grew as her cheeks warmed to a pretty pink. "Uh-oh. Did *you*?"

"I sure hope not," Brad said lightly, hoping she'd understand a little of what he was trying to tell her without coming right out and saying the words.

Judging by the rosy color of her fair complexion she was getting the idea that he was taking the show of affection seriously. It was way too soon for that, of course, but he knew no amount of reasoning was going to alter how he felt.

Either the following days would bring them closer or push them apart. Whatever happened, he knew he'd have to accept it. But he sure wasn't going to be happy if he was distanced from Janie.

Not one bit.

SIXTEEN

As the plane taxied off the runway, Janie peered out the closest window, expecting to spy a terminal and other planes. The lighted outline of the airstrip, itself, and several small hangars were all she could see.

The tail swung around. The hatch, a side section of fuselage with steps on it, lowered slowly. She waited with Pixie as Brad shook hands with the pilots and paused at the open doorway. The tension in his body was evident. Then he apparently spotted a friendly face because he waved and started down the ramp to the tarmac.

Damp, cool air swirled until the engines were stopped. Then there was silence except for the leftover gusts from the edges of the storm. Waiting for Brad's signal, Janie stood very still, listening, alert for any possible threat despite Brad's relaxed demeanor.

Finally, he turned and motioned to her. "Come on. I want you to meet my chief."

She clung to the railing with one hand and cradled her little pet with her other arm as she went down the stairs.

"Janie Kirkpatrick, meet Chief Wes Winterhaven," Brad said as she joined them.

"How do you do, sir?" Janie offered her hand and the chief shook it. He was a bit older than she'd imagined but since he had had a nearly adult son it made sense that he'd be middle-aged. Although he was in plain clothes instead of his uniform, his bearing identified him as a person who took charge and knew what he was doing. He could just as easily have been a retired military officer with his short gray hair and well-trimmed mustache.

"My pleasure. And please call me Wes. In the operation that's to follow we'll be on a first-name basis, anyway. The last thing I want to do is cause anyone to suspect I'm anything but a wealthy businessman."

"Of course."

Brad interrupted, "Where are we, anyway? The pilot mentioned the name Armbruster."

Janie's glance had drifted past the hangars to a brightly lit building perched on the crest of a hill in the distance. It reminded her of one of the modern mansions she'd seen on the covers of decorating magazines. If it was half as big and luxurious as it looked, it promised to be amazing.

"Yes," Wes said. "This place belongs to Harold Armbruster. We met in college, years ago, and have stayed friends. He and his wife, Meg, have a son about Wesley Jr.'s age."

Speaking that name caused the older man's smile to fade and his countenance darken. Janie remembered well the name of the teen whose murder Brad was trying to solve. No wonder the chief had gone to such lengths to discover who was behind that killing and probably others.

Brad looped an arm of comfort over Wes's shoulders and walked with him to a waiting limo. Janie followed. She wished she had nicer clothing but that couldn't be helped. Surely, there would be accommodations in that enormous mansion that would enable her to both clean up and appear less like a street urchin. That was certainly how she felt climbing into the back of the limousine with Brad and Wes.

A uniformed driver the size of a football linebacker held the door for them, then slid behind the wheel. She yearned to ask more questions, to hear about the plans for her and for Brad now that they were in a secure location, but she didn't want to disturb the men's thoughts.

She stared at Brad, waiting for him to notice. An arch of one eyebrow was his only reaction when he met her gaze. That, and a barely perceptible shake of his head was all the acknowledgment he gave.

Fine. She'd sit there like a useless bump

on a log for as long as it took. At this point there was no way she was giving anybody a reason to sideline her. She was in this up to her neck and intended to see it through to the end, whatever that turned out to be.

Her intrinsic awareness of the driver gave her a shiver. The man's eyes reflected in the mirror were dark and brooding. They matched the rest of his persona and it was unsettling.

So, how was she going to figure out who to believe and who to doubt?

Don't trust anybody came to her as clearly as if Brad had whispered it in her ear.

Janie shivered from her toes to the top of her head. *Don't trust any man* had been her motto from childhood and she had managed to cling to that without exception. Until she'd met Brad. Her heart and mind insisted he was the exception to her firm rule and she refused to argue the point. She was, however, suspicious of everyone else to some degree.

Did that include the police chief? she

asked herself. His role in their ongoing drama seemed innocent enough. It was his friends she felt most wary about. Them, and their minions, such as the chauffeur, who looked as though he could snap this limo in half without even breaking a sweat.

The luxury car followed a circular drive, stopping smoothly in front of a stone portico framed by square columns and containing an intricately carved door with eclectic patterns of stained glass inserts.

Janie stifled a gasp. "Oh, my!"

Brad agreed, "Yeah. What she just said." He turned to his chief as the driver opened the car door. "You actually went to school with this guy?"

Winterhaven nodded. "I did. Of course, I didn't know at the time how wealthy his family was. Unlike a lot of my classmates, he didn't flaunt it. After we graduated, I went on to the police academy and Harold came back to Missouri to join his father and brothers in the advertising business. Thanks to him, the company diversified from print into multimedia at just the right time."

"Earning enough to build a palace," Janie said softly, belatedly realizing she had spoken her thoughts aloud.

That brought a chuckle from Brad that made her blush as she grasped his offered hand and stepped out.

"Yeah," he said to Wes. "It looks like your friend can afford to send a private plane for us. I was kind of worried about that. I know it costs a lot."

The chief gave them a wistful smile. "He's promised to fund my—our—efforts to get to the bottom of things. I already mentioned some of our suspicions and he's acquainted with a few of the names on my list."

Brad voiced Janie's innermost thoughts. "I don't see how that can help. I mean, suspecting and being certain are very different things, not to mention proving anything."

Nodding support, Janie kept watching the chief's face and analyzing his responses, searching for warning signs. She saw none. Nor did she doubt Winterhaven's trust in his old friend. The problem was the outlying figures in this possible conspiracy. Who was going to vet them?

Together, the trio climbed the stone steps to the front entrance. Before they got to the door, it swung open. A portly gentleman wearing a cashmere sweater and obviously expensive loafers with fine wool slacks greeted them with open arms.

"Hello, hello, hello. Welcome. Any friends of Wes's are friends of mine." He swept his arm to the side and half bowed. "Please, come in. And call me Harold."

Brad and the chief stood back for Janie so she led the way, managing to offer a hand and shake Armbruster's without Pixie trying to nip him. "I'm Janie Kirkpatrick. How do you do?"

"My pleasure." His twinkling gray eyes seemed totally without guile. "I take it you're the courageous nurse who accidentally got mixed up in all of this."

She smiled in response to his praise. "It was a surprise but so far, so good."

"And more good to come, Lord willing," the older man said as he reached to greet the men. "Has Wes filled you in on our latest plan?"

Shaking her head, Janie noted that Brad looked confused, too. That wasn't terribly comforting. She'd have liked it better if he had at least known what they were getting into before agreeing to it. However, in retrospect, she could see that they hadn't had much of a choice, particularly with armed assassins waiting for them around every corner and behind every bush.

"Well, never mind that now," their host said. "I know you all must be tired and hungry. What will it be first? Food or sleep?"

Brad deferred to his chief and Janie to Brad. Wes took charge. "Let's get these agents a decent meal and then show them to their rooms," he said. "There'll be plenty of time for planning tomorrow."

Janie had to struggle to keep a wide grin

in check. The chief was equating her with Brad as if she, too, were a police officer. The notion was thrilling. Complimentary beyond imagination.

It was also frightening, particularly since she was now in unfamiliar territory both physically and emotionally. There was nothing in her upbringing or any of her professional training that equipped her to fit into this environment, let alone function so that she wouldn't attract undue attention.

Armbruster led the party through a formal dining room, opulent with crystal chandeliers and fresh flower arrangements setting off an enormous table and twelve chairs. Janie absently brushed at her worn clothing, hoping he wasn't going to invite them to sit at such a formal table.

The kitchen they then entered was mostly polished stainless steel and copper and appeared to be fit for any occasion from small family meals to preparing the grandest of banquets.

"Please, everyone, have a seat," Harold

said. He eyed Pixie. "Would you like me to have one of my people take care of that dog for you? They could walk her."

"Thank you for the offer. But I'd rather look after her myself. She's used to me." Janie flashed a glance at Brad. "To us."

"I see. Well, as long as my wife isn't here to object, it's fine with me if you keep her with you at the table."

Warmth of embarrassment rose on Janie's face, turning her cheeks rosier. "I am sorry. Really. Pixie needs me to take care of her."

The police chief elbowed Brad. "Sounds an awful lot like something you've said recently, if I recall."

It was evident, judging by the guarded expression on Brad's face and the cynicism on Wes's, that she was involved in that comparison even though her name hadn't been mentioned, and she decided to turn the tables on them.

"The main reason I agreed to fly up here was to keep looking after Brad the same as I do Pixie. I wanted to be handy if he needed more patching up."

Although Janie had intended to be funny, the thought of Brad being injured caused cold dread to spread through her. He was standing right there in front of her, yet she was already experiencing a sense of great loss.

SEVENTEEN

Brad didn't particularly appreciate Janie's insinuation that he'd needed her instead of the other way around, but he could understand why she'd made it. And, in a way, he had to agree. She had pulled him out of the figurative fire more than once. Of course he'd returned the favor, a fact he would fully explain the first chance he got to speak to Wes and Harold in private.

No doubt Janie was special. There was a feistiness to her that reminded him of the way her silly little dog tackled the world. Maybe that was why dog and master were so well suited to each other. He wondered which breed of dog would best complement him. Not that it mattered. In his line of work, having pets at home would be a distinct disadvantage.

The same thing went for having a family, Brad realized. Most of the cops who did marry reported difficulties. Not only did they face constant temptation, the spouse often felt physically and emotionally abandoned, not to mention the possibility of children growing up without the positive influence of two parents.

That was what had befallen Chief Westerhaven, Brad recalled. Wes and his ex-wife had shared custody of their only son, but the older the boy got, the less control Wes had over him. When Wesley Jr. had gotten in a bind with the drug scene and had begged his dad for help, it had already been too late.

Which was another reason why the chief was so determined. And why Brad had vowed to help his friend and mentor regardless of the sacrifices he'd have to make. The only aspect that wasn't fair was the involvement of the innocent nurse.

His gaze met Janie's across the kitchen

table. Their eyes locked and the rest of the room faded into insignificance. Brad reached toward her hand, realizing the distance was too great yet yearning to offer encouragement.

Instead of meeting his effort half-way, Janie got to her feet and purposely changed chairs. Once she was seated beside him she rested one hand on the edge of the table where he could easily reach it.

"I'm so sorry this is happening to you," Brad said quietly as he threaded his fingers between hers.

"It is what it is," she replied.

The trembling he had expected to feel was gone. So was the physical chill he'd felt a few times when he'd touched her during the flight. "You're really all right?"

She gave his hand a squeeze. "I am." A smile twitched the corners of her mouth. "When I'm with you, I'm more than all right. Don't ask me to explain it, I just feel safer."

"You're not all that safe when people are shooting at us," he countered.

"We're here. Together." Another squeeze. "We survived things that could have ended one or both of us. Yet they didn't. I, for one, am deeply grateful."

"And I owe you," Brad said tenderly. "A lot."

Chuckling, Wes interrupted, "Okay, you two. If the mutual admiration is finished, let's eat, shall we?" He looked to their host. "My thanks to Mr. Armbruster and his staff for providing such wonderful choices on short notice."

Brad passed the basket of bread first, then began to hand along plates of roast meats and cheeses that servers in aprons had placed there. Condiments sat in the center of the oval table in small crystal bowls and cruets.

A shiver at the nape of his neck caused him to eye the door. Two large men wearing tailored jackets had taken up positions on either side of the doorway. He turned to the opposite exit. It, too, was being guarded.

At his side, Brad felt Janie's elbow.

When he looked at her, she was nodding in the direction of the men he'd noticed. "Yes," he said. "I see them."

"They're good guys, right?"

"They have to be," Brad told her.

"You're sure?"

Janie's doubt reinforced his own. Yes, they were supposed to be on safe ground there. But his instincts were not convinced. Normally he'd have credited his unease to the trials they'd experienced in order to reach the estate. In this case, however, he tended to trust Janie's senses as well as his own. Given her reluctance to simply accept the situation and let down her guard, he wouldn't do so, either.

Leaning closer to whisper in her ear, Brad said, "Time will tell."

She turned to face him. "That's what I was afraid you'd say."

Their eyes met. So close despite the others at the table and the servants and bodyguards in the background.

All he'd have to do is lean a few inches closer and he could kiss her. Again.

Long seconds passed. Time slowed. Brad hardly breathed. Then he began to turn his head away.

In his peripheral vision he caught a slight movement. Janie had moved, too, only not away from him.

He felt her soft lips brush his cheek, the caress of her warm breath against his skin. If he'd been a split second slower she'd have actually kissed him—in front of all these people!

The thought brought an unwelcome blush and a tenuous smile as Brad looked around the table. Wes and Harold were averting their glances and ostensibly concentrating on their food. But they had seen.

Releasing Janie's hand, Brad picked up his sandwich and took a bite. It might as well have been made of cardboard because he hardly tasted it.

In his mind, despite all his efforts to the contrary, he was reliving her innocent kiss and remembering what it had felt like when he had kissed her to silence her outside the hospital.

That was different, he insisted. He'd only done it because he hadn't wanted to clamp his hand over her mouth to quiet her down. *Yeah, right,* his conscience countered. *You did exactly what you wanted to do.*

He shrugged, continuing to eat. Any affection he had shown Janie when they were away from known acquaintances actually had been different. Then, nobody who mattered would have observed their emotional connection or guessed how much they meant to each other. Here and now, they were on a totally different playing field.

That's what it was, Brad concluded. An arena. With unknown players and very little defense on their team. Wes, he trusted. And perhaps Armbruster, too, although that was still to be proven.

He cast a sidelong glance at the bodyguards. They were the largest unknown factor. Brad's experience as a cop had shown him that some allegiances were deeper and stronger than money, no matter how much cash was involved. Almost anyone could be bought but that was no guarantee that they would remain true to the one who paid them under every circumstance.

Therefore, the men stationed at each door might be there to defend him and his companions, which was his fondest wish.

Otherwise, they could be meant to keep anyone from escaping.

Janie managed to be a tiny bit embarrassed for her show of affection but that didn't mean she was sorry she'd kissed Brad's cheek. Granted, the location for the kiss was not the wisest. Nor was Janie sure Brad hadn't taken offense, although his lack of a negative response cheered her.

The two older men made short work of their impromptu meal while Brad only ate part of his sandwich and she managed to down even less of hers, feeding little bites of meat to her dog out of sight below the tabletop. Janie credited her lack of hunger to the candy bar she'd eaten shortly before landing, because nervousness normally led her straight to the refrigerator, usually including ice cream.

That thought brought a smile. A sense that Brad was looking at her made her swivel to share her mood. The twitch at the corners of his mouth cheered her.

She mouthed a barely spoken, "Sorry."

"No problem."

"You aren't mad?"

That softened his expression even more. "No. I'm not mad at you."

She pantomimed wiping sweat from her forehead. "Whew. That's a relief."

Harold Armbruster interrupted by clearing his throat. "Excuse me, folks. If everyone is through eating, I think it's time we turned in. The next few days are going to be busy."

Rising first, Harold led the way back to the opulent entry with its cascading crystal chandeliers and a grand, sweeping staircase that reminded Janie of those she'd seen in movies. It had polished hardwood stairs and a curving banister that led to a landing halfway up, then split to the right and left to continue to the second floor.

"Ladies to the right, gentlemen to the left," their host said. "Ms. Kirkpatrick, there is a maid waiting to make you and your dog comfortable. Please don't hesitate to ask for whatever you want."

"Thank you." Janie nodded to him. It was comforting to climb the wide staircase next to Brad and his chief and hard to part at the landing. Still, she knew she had to leave them. Pausing, she rested Pixie on her hip and reached for Brad's hand. "Be…be careful."

"You, too. See you in the morning."

She managed a slight smile. "God willing."

"I'm counting on that," Brad said with a squeeze of her hand. "He brought us this far."

"I think He brought us together in the

first place," Janie said. "I don't see our meeting as a mistake at all."

Another warm, brief squeeze before he released her. "I'm glad. Maybe, in the end, I'll be able to agree."

Janie's smile widened to a grin. "You may as well give up and agree with me now. You know I'm always right."

It thrilled her to see his dark eyes twinkling in the light from the chandeliers. "You do have your moments of genius," he said quietly.

"Just moments?"

She was still smiling at him when he wished her a good night, and accompanied the men up the other branch of the stairway. Alone on the landing except for Pixie, she suddenly felt very vulnerable. That was silly, of course. After all, they were the guests of a friend of a friend, one whose reputation was apparently stellar and who had gone out of his way to welcome them into his home.

A shiver spurred her to dash up the last portion of the stairway. Once she reached the second floor she saw only one door standing open. That had to be her room.

Or a trap, she countered, ashamed of herself for letting her imagination have free rein.

"I'm safe. I'm fine," she repeated, approaching the doorway.

The great house was silent. Her footsteps on the plush carpeting in the upper hallway didn't make a sound.

"Ma'am?" a dark-haired young woman asked from the open doorway.

Janie jumped, making Pixie yip. She was surprised to see the woman wearing casual clothing instead of the expected uniform, but her servant's demeanor identified her as the promised maid. "You startled me," Janie said.

"My apologies, ma'am. Are you ready for sleep or a warm bath?"

"Um, no." Janie eyed her dog. "I'll need to walk Pixie before I turn in. Can you direct me to a good place? A safe place?"

"Of course, ma'am."

"My name is Janie." She smiled at the

maid. "When you call me ma'am it makes me feel ancient."

That brought out a demure smile. "I'm Nancy."

"Hello, Nancy. Pleased to meet you."

"And you, ma—Janie. I've laid out a choice of nightclothes and several other outfits that should suit you for daywear until Mrs. Armbruster has a chance to shop for you. I'll see what other appropriate things I can come up with in the meantime. Shoes, especially. Do you like sandals?"

"When I'm not working, yes," Janie said. "I'm afraid I've had to leave behind everything, including a leash for Pixie. Is there a belt or sash I can use?"

"How about the adjustable shoulder strap from a small handbag? I'm sure I can find you one of those with a clip on it."

"Sounds perfect. Thanks."

"Will it be all right if we meet at the base of the stairs? I'll have to check storage for the strap."

"Of course," Janie said before thinking it through.

"Be there in a sec," Nancy told her, bustling past.

Still clinging to Pixie, Janie slowly retraced her steps and descended the staircase. The little dog was trembling, her black eyes wide, nose quivering. Something was wrong. Janie knew it.

Dark and quiet, the immense foyer seemed to be closing in on her. Shadows lengthened. Lights dimmed. Gusts of wind left from the passing storm crept into crevices and made the house moan.

She stopped. Listened. Silently reached out to God when words failed her. She knew she was not imagining the sense of menace. It was there as surely as it had been when they'd fled the black SUVs or dodged bullets.

"Only this time it's subtle," Janie mused, peering into corners. "And I don't like subtle. Not one little bit."

"Excuse me?"

Janie jumped as if hit by one of the lightning bolts they'd flown by. Pixie growled.

A man stepped out of a shadowy doorway. There was something slightly familiar about him.

He paused, studying her. "Sorry to scare you, Janie."

"Do…do I know you?"

A tilt of his head substituted for a greeting. "You should. I'm Rick. I was flying your plane."

Ah, the copilot. "Sorry. I hadn't expected to see you again."

The grin he gave her was reminiscent of a contented cat with feathers on its chin from a recently purloined meal. "You'll see a lot of me, I imagine. I work here."

Janie hoped her feigned attitude of nonchalance was good enough to fool the man because encountering him here, in the same house, was anything but comforting.

"How nice for you," she said with a plastic smile. "Good night, then."

"Good night."

And just like that he was gone, back the

way he'd come before running into her in the foyer. Before she had time to work herself up into a state, Nancy reappeared, bouncing down the stairs with her find.

"Got you a temporary leash," the girl said, grinning. "Will this do?"

"It's perfect." Janie mirrored the smile. "Are you coming with us?"

"Oh. Well, I suppose I could if you need me, but…"

"I'd like the company, if you don't mind."

"I was told to make you feel at home, and if you want me to walk outside with you, I don't see why not." She led the way off to her left. "Come on. I'll show you a side door. It'll be quicker and easier."

"Wonderful." Following, Janie felt as if a ton of weight had lifted off her shoulders. Not that having Nancy by her side would be any real protection, it just made her feel better to have a companion.

Only after they were outside did it occur to her that she was now responsible for taking care of the younger woman, too.

That put her on full alert and caused her to search the shadows next to the house and ornamental shrubbery. Every little twitch of a leaf or movement of a branch sent her senses into overdrive.

Janie was surprised to see Nancy crossing her arms against the chill, reflecting her own nervousness.

There was no doubt. They both sensed danger.

EIGHTEEN

Brad was exhausted. So why was sleep eluding him? He'd been shown to a private room that overlooked a swath of lawn that sloped down from the far side of the easternmost wing. Yard lights apparently had been left on to increase security because he could see almost as well as during an overcast day. Yes, there were pools of darkness but overall the artificial illumination served its purpose.

Directly below his window a section of grass suddenly grew brighter, as if someone had opened a door and let light pour out. Even with his forehead against the pane he couldn't see what was going on until a slim human shadow blocked the beams. He wouldn't have dreamed he was seeing Janie if the shadow hadn't been attached to a small, wiggly figure at its feet. Plus, there was someone unknown with them.

"Janie?" Brad scowled. *What is she up to?*

The taller of the two human figures was highlighted enough that he could see Janie's fair hair. It almost looked haloed. She had proceeded down a short set of steps, then ventured out onto the lawn. Brad couldn't take his eyes off her. His hands fisted. His pulse sped. Yes, she seemed okay, but no, he didn't like her being out there. Pixie was not adequate protection, and if she thought her other companion was going to be any help, she was fooling herself.

There was only one thing for him to do. Stopping to slip his shoes back on, he grabbed his jacket off a clothes tree and headed for the stairs. There was enough light for him to take them two at a time. He hit the floor at the bottom with his hand on the newel post and used it as a pivot point, swinging around until he was headed in the right direction before letting go.

He wasn't sure where to find the closest exit but he intended to try. Yes, he could have left via the main front door but he figured it would take him just as long to race around the spacious ground-floor exterior as it would to find the door Janie had used.

An open floor plan made it easier to locate French doors in a nearby anteroom. Those opened onto a garden Brad assumed was the one he'd seen from above.

He slowed just enough to quietly ease open one of the glass grid-work panels and step through, then made straight for the lawn. There was nobody there! Not Janie, not her dog, not even the extra person he'd spotted with them. Was he in the wrong place?

A quick glance up at the second story showed bright light shining from his room. He was off by a little. Rounding a hedge with long strides, he finally saw her.

"Janie!"

She not only didn't react, she was behaving strangely. So was her companion. Pixie, however, was her usual self, barking and straining at the end of a short leash.

Closing the distance, Brad tried again, "Janie! Over here."

The woman whirled. The dog did not. High-pitched yips and yaps echoed off the sides of the mansion.

Brad was beside them in seconds. He opened his arms and Janie stepped into his embrace. A young, dark-haired woman backed off instead.

"It's okay, Nancy," Janie told her. "He's a friend."

"Then what's over there?" The maid edged closer.

"I don't know," Janie answered. She lifted her face to Brad's. "We heard something moving. I might have thought it was all in our imagination if Pixie hadn't alerted."

"Stay here. I'll go check it out."

"No way."

"I should have known you'd be trouble. When will you learn to trust me?"

"I do trust you," Janie countered.

"Not enough to listen to my advice." Brad eyed the other woman. "Nancy, is it? Keep her here." He brandished the better of the two guns they'd taken from the thugs. "I'm armed, as you can see. And Janie is not."

"A-all right."

"A sensible woman for a change," Brad muttered, starting away. Behind him he heard Janie arguing with Nancy. It was impossible to tell who was winning but he figured that anything that delayed her from trailing after him was a plus.

Illumination from the house and yard lights made seeing into the darker fringes more difficult. Except for the voices of the women, he heard nothing. Nor was anyone lurking as they had suspected. Still, it wouldn't hurt to check more closely. He just hoped Armbruster's bodyguards didn't mistake him for a prowler and shoot before asking questions.

Three more yards. Ten. Fifteen. Brad rounded a corner of the house that was bordered by lush vegetation and set off by an arbor of some kind. He hoped it was grapevines because he wasn't keen on tangling with rose thorns.

Something moved to his right. Brad froze. He suddenly realized the noisy argument had stopped. Silence reigned. Could the women—could Janie—be in trouble? Had he made the wrong choice by leaving her?

Brad whirled. Peered into the distance, listening for any whisper of sound that would set his heart and mind at ease.

Nothing. He raised the gun, his elbow bent, and pointed it at the sky as he started back to where he'd left Janie.

He'd just reached the corner he'd rounded earlier when he felt a jolt. Sensed pain. Faltered and dropped to his knees before falling forward, facedown.

In the distance someone screamed.

Then his field of vision narrowed, ending in a single point of light that winked out like a distant star on a cloudy night.

Janie thrust the leash at Nancy and began to run toward Brad. She was unarmed. But it didn't matter, not when somebody needed her nursing skills. She hadn't actually witnessed the blow that had felled him but she'd certainly heard something connect with his head an instant before she saw him fall.

Her hand pressed on his shoulder. "Hold still." He was moving but groggy, which was a good sign. "Please, Brad, don't move."

"The gun," he mumbled.

Janie expertly scooped it up, engaged the safety the way he'd taught her, then slipped it into the back of her waistband to free her hands, placing both on his shoulders. "I've got it. Now stop wiggling and let me check you over."

"We need to get back in the house," Brad insisted, raising on one elbow.

The increasing steadiness of his voice

helped calm her. "In a second. I don't want you getting up too soon and crashing again." She motioned to Nancy. "I need your help."

The maid came with Pixie in tow and the little dog sniffed Brad for a second before licking his cheek. He chuckled low, then grimaced. "Ow."

"This is a bigger whack than what you got on the plane," Janie told him. "It's gonna hurt."

"Yeah. Figured that out for myself. Did you see who hit me?"

"No." Janie looked up. "Nancy? Did you see anything?"

"Just him, falling on his face," the maid said. Her eyes kept darting nervously as she searched their surroundings.

"Okay." Janie had checked Brad's neck and briefly examined his scalp. Whatever he'd been hit with was, fortunately, blunt instead of sharp. "We need to get ice on your head before the goose egg swells any more. It's already noticeable."

She got ready to help him up when Brad

tried to spring to his feet and faltered. Janie righted him. "What part of taking it slow did you not understand?" she asked cynically.

"I'm fine. You don't need to baby me."

"Then try to keep your balance and let's go." Janie motioned to Nancy. "Bring Pixie and walk on Brad's other side, just in case."

"I told you, I'm fine."

"I'll be the judge of that." She clenched her jaw as he leaned a little too heavily on her. "I hope you don't need an MRI or a CAT scan because I have no idea how far it is to the nearest hospital."

"No hospitals. Period."

Janie realized he was staring sideways at her when he asked, "How would anybody know you were out here? Were you followed?"

"I don't think so but I wasn't really watching. I did run into our copilot in the foyer while I was waiting for Nancy to find me a leash."

Janie looked past Brad to Nancy. "He said his name was Rick."

"Rick Evans. He hasn't worked here long, maybe three or four months."

"Interesting," Brad said.

Janie could tell he was recovering his strength and balance quickly but she kept hold of his upper arm just the same, feeling his muscles flexing beneath her fingers. Honesty forced her to admit she was enjoying the situation a bit too much. Guilt finally convinced her to let go.

They climbed the two short steps to the side door together. Brad held the door for the women, then followed them inside despite Janie's initial insistence that he go first.

Lights were dim in that section of the house so Janie pointed toward the kitchen. "Everybody go that way. I'll need light and a first-aid kit. Nancy, can you get one for us?"

"Sure. No problem. Back in a sec."

Staying with Brad, Janie watched to make sure her dog was following them.

Sweet little Pixie seemed determined not to let either human out of her sight and was tagging along in a zigzag motion, leash and all, as if herding disobedient sheep.

Janie pulled out a kitchen chair and ordered, "Sit."

Brad sat. "You sure get bossy when somebody needs first aid, don't you?"

"It's my job," she said, stepping closer to the sink and pulling down a fistful of paper towels. "If Mr. Armbruster has a doctor on call the way he seems to have every other profession, he may be able to look you over. I'd hate to be wrong and have you keel over on me because of a misdiagnosis."

"Haven't you figured out by now that I trust you completely?"

Coming to stand behind his chair, Janie began to clean around his head wound with the wet paper towels. "Trust is fine but expertise is something else entirely. I'm not qualified to diagnose your injury and I'd feel a lot better about it if we got a second opinion."

Brad reached up without looking and grasped one of her wrists, then pulled her around to face him. "If it seems necessary, I promise I'll ask for further care."

The touch of his fingers clasping her wrist and his thumb caressing her pulse point nearly pushed first aid out of her mind. She hesitated. Resisted. Then melted as if she were a lighted candle and the room a furnace.

"Please. Let me take care of you."

"You've already done more than I can ever thank you for," he said, speaking softly. As he stood, Janie tried to step back, give ground, but his hold on her wrist prevented it.

Despite the fact that they were in unfamiliar surroundings and still on edge from the attack outside, Janie felt an emotional pull unlike any she'd experienced before.

Feelings were not to be trusted, she reminded herself. Feelings, particularly for men, could get you in terrible trouble.

Could hurt you. Could betray your trust the way her brothers and her alcoholic father had.

But this was Brad, Janie reasoned. He was different, at least he had been so far, and she couldn't help seeing him as the antithesis of her abusive, unloving family.

As if belonging in his arms, she eased forward. He let go of her wrist and she slipped both arms around his waist.

He drew her in lovingly. Janie breathed a sigh and laid her cheek against his chest.

When he finally spoke she could hear a quaver in his voice. "You have to promise me to be more careful. I don't want to lose you. Please?"

Nodding, she meant the unspoken vow with all her heart, yet she also knew she would continue to do everything she could to look after him. Whatever it took.

Standing there together, Janie found temporary peace and sent up a silent prayer of thanks. In the midst of conflict it was hard to remember to pray except perhaps a quick, desperate plea for immediate aid. In the aftermath of a crisis she always tried to give thanks, particularly while on the job.

This situation, however, differed in so many ways it made her mind spin. She was out of her element most of the time. If Brad hadn't been injured several times she'd have had no use for her medical training and she certainly didn't intend to celebrate that.

Thankfully, she possessed other skills and was learning more by the minute. Martial arts had helped several times and now that she'd become a little more comfortable handling firearms, she'd been able to fall back on that when she'd defended Brad boarding the plane and safely retrieved the gun he'd dropped that night.

As Janie continued to rest her cheek on his shoulder, she wondered what other harrowing events awaited them. That unspoken question bothered her enough to ask, "Will you promise me the same thing? You'll be careful?"

"Yes."

His low voice vibrated beneath her ear and its timbre made her shiver. While she was enfolded in this man's embrace, it seemed as if all was well, regardless of what went on around them. That was foolish, she knew. And could actually be dangerous if either of them let down their guard. Still, this was where she wanted to be. Who she wanted to be with.

What about after their tasks were complete? her heart asked. What would happen when it was safe for her to go home to Springfield and Brad no longer needed her?

She wanted to ask, to raise her face to his and boldly question his intentions, yet she didn't move a muscle for fear it would cause him to release her. How long could they stand there like that? How long did she dare remain close enough for him to guess her innermost yearnings? Was he going to hold her that way forever? That notion certainly appealed.

"Got it!" Nancy announced, bursting into the kitchen.

Brad jumped back and Janie had her answer. Their stolen moments of tenderness and intrinsic connection were over. For now. Blushing, she accepted the first-aid kit and went to work.

Although she was as gentle as possible with all her patients, she knew the touch of her fingers this time was different. It was tender, yes, but so much more. Did Brad sense the change, the deepening of her emotional commitment? Janie hoped not, because if he did, she was afraid he'd be more liable to take chances on her behalf. To risk too much.

Her breath caught, stuttering. She could not lose the only man she'd been able to trust since childhood. She simply could not.

NINETEEN

Sporting a small bandage and nursing a splitting headache, Brad joined Wes, Janie and Harold Armbruster in the expansive kitchen for breakfast that morning. He'd already spoken with the chief about the latest assault, and they had decided to downplay it until they'd sorted out a few disturbing details.

"Morning." Brad accepted a cup of steaming coffee from a server and added cream from a small pitcher at the table.

"What's with your head?" Armbruster asked.

Brad quickly grasped Janie's hand and squeezed it to keep her from commenting. "Just clumsy. I must have banged it harder than I thought when I went sliding around in your plane."

"Humph. Didn't notice it last night."

"Yeah. I guess it opened up when I took a shower." A sidelong glance at Janie telegraphed further warning and Brad could tell she'd picked up on his cues because her fingers tightened around his.

"Need stitches?"

"Naw," Brad said, smiling to keep the mood light and to project nonchalance. "I'm good. Our resident nurse bandaged it up for me last night."

"Was it you we heard moving around outside? That little dog sure can bark."

"Sorry," Janie said. "I needed to walk Pixie and she loves to chase everything from blowing leaves to butterflies."

"No problem. Where is the monster mutt this morning?"

"Nancy's watching her. I love Pixie but she makes it hard for me to enjoy visiting when she demands so much attention."

"That's good," Wes piped up. "You'll

need someplace safe to leave her during the party."

"Party?"

Brad had been planning to fill Janie in about the upcoming covert operation when they had a little more privacy. Now that Wes had brought it up he changed his mind. "It's a cocktail party that Wes and Harold have arranged. We'll have a few days to get ourselves ready."

Janie looked panicked. "I have nothing to wear!"

Armbruster chuckled. "Not to worry, my dear. My Meg'll take care of all that."

Brad explained, "His wife has been shopping in New York but she's expected back tomorrow. If you'll give her your size, Harold says she'll pick up something special for you, too."

"Oh, dear." Janie gave Brad a pleading look. "Can't I just stay upstairs?"

Chief Winterhaven interrupted, "I'd rather you mix and mingle, Janie. You and Brad are the only ones who have seen some of the gang members and we're hoping you'll be able to identify them."

"They aren't coming to the party, are they?"

"Not as guests. But these people are, for the most part, wealthy and cautious. We expect them to bring bodyguards and other staff with them. Those are the ones we especially want you to look at."

"But they'll recognize us, too," Janie blurted out.

Brad's hold on her hand tightened and he willed her to concentrate on his explanation. "Harold promises that we won't look like ourselves and I believe him. I'll be getting a haircut and they'll have a crew do a makeover on you. Show up in fancy clothes in a different setting and we should be able to pull this off. At least long enough to figure out who works for who."

"That will tell us which major criminal groups are involved," Wes explained. "We already know the identities of lower echelon players, like Speevey and his sons.

What we're looking for is a connection between them and someone who gives the orders."

And had Wesley Jr. killed, Brad filled in, unspoken. Which was information he'd been charged to get while undercover. If he had succeeded, none of this would have been necessary.

Mulling over his failure, Brad was suddenly struck by the realization that if he'd managed to learn more while in Springfield he might never have met Janie Kirkpatrick. It was his concern for Tim that had brought them together, and since then nearly everything had kept them close. Perhaps she'd been right when she'd surmised that God meant for them to be acquainted. That didn't prove anything, but it was an interesting premise.

One other element had been weighing on Brad's mind and he decided to express his concern. Although he would have preferred to have discussed it with Wes first, he decided to take advantage of this opportunity.

He looked to their host. "I take it you've prepared a guest list and given it to the chief?"

"I have. I've also instructed my people to copy background files and make them available."

Brad sensed that his inquiry had offended Armbruster but he had one more thing to ask. "What about your son? Will he be there, too?"

"Chase?" The older man huffed. "I suppose so, if he's back in time. He's been vacationing in the Caribbean for months." He addressed Wes, "Do you want me to invite him? I'd thought, Chase being such close friends with your boy, you might prefer not to see him right now."

Careful observation failed to tell Brad how his chief actually felt but Wes did manage an amiable smile. "Nonsense. The boy belongs with his parents. If he's ready to come home, by all means, let him."

"All right, then. I'll have my secretary make the arrangements. I'm sure Chase can be back by Friday night."

"Good," Wes said. To Brad, the chief looked weary and sad in spite of the grin pasted on his face. If he hadn't known him so well, he might have been fooled, but clearly the man was still grieving. Deeply.

Janie's foot connected solidly with Brad's shin, getting his full attention. He raised an eyebrow at her.

"Um, as soon as we're done eating, I think I should check your bandage. And maybe you can go with me when I walk Pixie again?"

"Sure." He looked to his chief. "That won't be a problem, will it?"

"Not at all," Wes said, cheering Brad more than he'd expected and bringing on an easy smile.

"Okay," Janie said. "I'll head upstairs to get Pixie and meet you in fifteen."

"Same place?" Brad asked, hoping the others at the table and the observant serving staff didn't take too much notice.

"Perfect." She headed for the doorway leading to the foyer and staircase. As Brad watched her go, he marveled at how athletic and graceful she was. Remembering the healing in her gentle touch as well as the strength behind her martial arts moves, he felt a surge of appreciation for all she was and had been to him.

The notion that there was a lot more for them to experience together in the near future was definitely encouraging.

It also scared him to death.

TWENTY

Janie didn't waste much time getting ready to walk her dog. She'd already brushed her hair and put on a little lip gloss before breakfast so now all she had to do was freshen it.

"Thanks for watching Pixie," she told Nancy.

"It was fun. She's sure full of energy. I had to chase her all over your room after she stole a sock."

Laughing, Janie opened her arms to Pixie. "Come here, girl. Have you been teasing poor Nancy?"

The little white dog reacted as if Janie had just told her she was the best dog in the whole world.

"Will you be needing anything else this morning?" Nancy asked.

"Not that I know of." Janie's smile waned. "Mrs. Armbruster is supposed to buy me a cocktail dress in New York and that really bothers me. Is there something suitable wherever you've been finding these other nice clothes you've loaned me?"

Nancy eyed her up and down. "Maybe. Mrs. A keeps a pretty extensive wardrobe for her visiting nieces and nephews, just in case they don't bring the proper clothes for whatever is going on here." She lowered her eyes and stared at the carpet as if pondering before raising her gaze and explaining, "It's common knowledge so I guess it's okay to mention it. Mrs. Armbruster didn't come from money the way Mr. Armbruster did. A lot of her kin are shocked when they see how she lives and she tries to make their visits as pleasant and easy as possible. She's really a sweetheart."

"Thanks. That does make me feel better."

"You're welcome. As I said, my job is to make you comfortable. What colors do you favor? Design? Cocktail length? Longer? Give me some hints."

"Just pick out whatever you think might fit and I'll try them on. I'm not choosy." Janie glanced at her image in the mirrored closet doors. "I'm so used to living in plain scrubs for work and jeans at home that anything else seems glamorous."

Smiling, Janie enjoyed Nancy's soft chuckle as the maid said, "Okay. I promise to have a few dresses to choose from by lunchtime. I'll hang them in your closet. If you need help with zippers, just pick up the phone and somebody will buzz me."

"Do you carry a cell phone?" Janie asked.

Nancy produced a small one from an apron pocket. "Sure do. Want to call me that way?"

"I'd really rather keep it between the two of us," Janie said. "Less complicated that way."

"Works for me." Nancy held out her own

phone. "Pass me yours and put your number in mine if you want."

"Perfect." It truly was, Janie mused. She had decided to trust this amiable young woman and keeping any communications to a minimum would reinforce her convictions that she had nothing to fear. It would also allow her to ask for help in other areas, should she need it.

It was comforting to think she had another true ally in the house. Naturally Brad came first, then Chief Winterhaven, followed by Nancy. A small, trustworthy group was better than a larger one that gave evil a chance to infiltrate.

"Like my family," Janie muttered, belatedly realizing she had spoken aloud.

The maid looked up from the phone screen. "Beg pardon?"

"Never mind. I was just thinking." She paused, coloring. "My childhood wasn't the happiest."

"Whose was?"

That eased Janie's mind enough for a nod and a smile. "You're right. I suppose it's a matter of perspective. I just wonder what it might have been like to grow up in a home like this."

Eyebrows arching, Nancy shrugged. "I don't think that matters. I really don't. Look at Chase."

"Sorry?"

"Chase Armbruster. He always had everything his heart desired and I don't think he's one bit happier than I am. He's really been depressed since, well, you know."

"Sorry, I don't know what you mean." Janie waited.

"Since his best friend died. You know. Wesley Winterhaven, Junior. I figured, since you're a friend of the chief, you'd know the whole story."

"Maybe you should tell me your version," Janie said. "The more I know, the more help I can be to everybody."

"Well..."

Janie could understand Nancy's reluctance to tell tales, yet, as she'd said, the more detail she had, the more likely she'd be to spot inconsistencies in others. Including the main parties, she added, a bit chagrinned. That might mean she would eventually distrust Chief Winterhaven, although she figured that if Brad believed him, she should, too. Waiting, patient and silent, she let Nancy decide.

"Okay," the maid finally said. "The way I understand it, Wes and Chase were pretty close friends, like their fathers are. And you know how wild teenage boys can get. You had brothers."

Janie just nodded.

"I heard the boys were experimenting with drugs, got in too deep and felt trapped. Chase backed off and left the country. Wes contacted his father to ask for help getting away from the drug scene and ended up dead." She blushed. "Forgive me if that's too blunt but that's what happened. Do you know how come the chief is here now?"

"I may, but I can't share any details with anybody until I get permission. You understand, right?"

"I guess." The maid made a face. "I

know there are politics and favoritism in most families but this one takes the cake. No wonder Chase split for the Caribbean and his mother went shopping in New York."

"This all happened around the time of Wesley Jr.'s murder?"

"Chase left then. Mrs. A has only been gone a couple of weeks. She may actually be shopping, although I don't remember her ever being away for quite this long before."

"They'll both be back home for the party, as far as I know. Forgive me for asking, but do you and Chase have a thing going?"

"What? No way! That guy is nuts. Moody, you know?"

"Are there any other tips you can give me?"

Nancy chuckled behind her hand. "Not that I'd care to share. Being part of the staff is altogether different than being a guest, like you."

"Yes," Janie said. "I can tell. The trouble

is, I feel a lot more comfortable hanging around with you than I will socializing at this party coming up. If you see me edging toward the door, don't get in my way. I may be trying to escape."

They shared a laugh, quieting when Pixie got excited and started circling in front of the door.

"That's my cue," Janie said.

"If you're worried about going out alone, I can come."

"It shouldn't be necessary in the daylight. Besides, Brad is meeting me."

"Ah!"

"Stop looking at me like that. We're just friends."

"That's the best starting place for a romance," Nancy offered. "If you decide you don't want him, let me know, okay? He's really good-looking."

"It's his good heart I love most," Janie said, realizing her slip of the tongue as soon as she uttered it. Although the friendly maid didn't comment, Janie could see that she'd taken note. This was not the time for relationships to blossom. The atmosphere was too tense, too unpredictable.

In truth, Janie likened her feelings about Brad to the flight during the lightning storm. There were blindingly bright instances and a roller-coaster ride of emotions to rival that of any amusement park. Being near him made her shaky, yet comforted. Fearful, yet courageous. Unsure, yet strongly motivated.

I don't love him, she insisted to herself.

A contradictory *Yes, I do* followed immediately and left her so tense she wanted to shout.

Instead, she scooped up her dog and left for their planned rendezvous, skipping down the stairs so rapidly she nearly missed a step.

Haste seemed called for, although she had no idea why the urge to hurry was so strong. Perhaps it was remembering the image of Brad, injured and sprawled on his face in the grass, that spurred her on.

Janie made a dash for the French doors and kept running until she spotted him.

He saw her coming and turned to face her.

She never slowed. His arms parted. And she sailed into his embrace, dog and all, like a battered ship seeking safe harbor from a storm.

Because Brad had had time to inspect the area and make sure there were no hidden threats, he felt comfortable embracing Janie. It hadn't surprised him when she'd run to him without hesitation. He'd known she would. And he'd known he should not encourage her, yet he had responded to her rapid, joyful approach as if they were a couple in love.

His hands lightly patted her back. She allowed her wiggling dog to jump down and laid her cheek against his chest. Brad was certain she could hear the pounding of his heart and would suspect that he cared for her. Should he move their relationship to the next level?

No. There was no doubt he wanted to but he had a duty to his chief. And to Janie. Revealing his personal feelings would only muddy the waters and become a distraction when what he needed was clarity of thought and strength of purpose.

He grasped her shoulders and set her away, seeing puzzlement in her expression and unshed moisture in her shining eyes. "Let's walk with your dog and get a little farther from the house so we can speak freely."

"Okay." Janie watched Pixie roaming close by.

"No leash today?"

"She'll come when I call her. This place is still unfamiliar territory so she's not likely to be too brave." Janie took a deep breath of the rain-washed air and sighed. "It's beautiful out here, isn't it?"

"I guess so." He shrugged. "I tend to see any place where I'm working as a battle-field. Luxury has nothing to do with it."

"That's sad."

"No," he said firmly, "it's survival.

You'd be wise to keep in mind that being here is like tiptoeing through a minefield. We don't know who our friends are, except for each other and Wes."

"Is that why you stopped me from talking at breakfast? You didn't want Armbruster to know you'd been hurt a second time?"

"Among other things, yes." His jaw muscles clenched and unclenched as he went on, "I know Wes trusts the man but I keep getting bad vibes."

"Maybe that's because of that shady copilot I ran into again last night."

"Maybe. Wes tells me the servants' wing houses all the regular employees with room for temps, too. I may do a little poking around later. See what clues I can turn up."

"Need a lookout?" Janie was smiling at him and he almost said yes.

"No, thanks. I can manage. I'll find out when Chase is expected home and plan my activities around what happens then. I assume somebody will go pick him up and maybe fly him home from the international airport."

"Smart." Her grin widened. "And sneaky."

"I'm trying." The satisfaction he received from her praise was out of balance with his usual reality but he figured that was no reason to stop enjoying it.

When Janie laughed and said, "Very trying," he had to join her. Once again her wit had lightened his mood and improved his outlook. What might it be like to be around her all the time?

As they strolled across the well-manicured lawn, Brad took Janie's hand. Her fingers slipped between his as naturally as if they had been holding hands for years. His senses heightened, making him keenly aware of her every nuance. Somehow, he kept imagining that she cared for him as much as he cared for her. Maybe even more.

That idea was both uplifting and frightening because it might mean she cared too much to behave rationally. He huffed.

Janie stopped and tugged on his hand. "What?"

"I was just thinking."

"About the case?"

"Actually, no. I was wasting my time worrying about whether you might react in a way that would put you in danger because of me, and it occurred to me that I already knew how far you'd go."

"Really?"

"Yeah, really. The things you've tackled lately are enough to send most women into hysterics. Instead, you crashed your car and shot at my enemies and even picked up a real gun to lay covering fire so I could get to safety."

"Guess I'm pretty cool, huh?"

Brad squeezed her fingers as he laughed softly, and nodded. "Yeah, you're amazing."

Reaching up with his free hand, he touched the bandage on his head. "Can I take this off now?"

"I think so, unless you're planning to

get in more trouble trying to protect me like last night."

Levity vanished, replace by poignant truth as Brad faced her and said, "I will do whatever I have to in order to keep you safe, no matter what. I promise."

The bang and high-pitched whine of a rifle bullet echoed out of nowhere! Brad dived for Janie, throwing himself on top of her, knocking her down and using his body as a human shield.

She screamed. Shouts in the distance began and drew closer. Estate guards were responding, late but welcome.

Holding Janie and praying for deliverance, Brad hardly felt it when Pixie bit his ankle.

His thoughts focused like a laser beam marking a target for a sharpshooter. *Why? How?* And most important, *Who?*

TWENTY-ONE

In the confusion following being shot at, it was easy to see that Brad had saved her life. As he had promised. And as he had done in the past. He might believe Janie was taking care of him but nobody could deny that it went both ways.

By the time she'd been interviewed by the police, Armbruster and his guards, Wes and Brad, she was numb. Facts blurred in her weary mind, leaving more questions than answers. Who had this gunman been after? Her? Brad? Wes? Or anybody connected with the Armbrusters? Anything was possible as well as plausible, a conclusion which provided no peace whatsoever.

The only thing that did distract her from

worrying about the attack was worrying about the upcoming cocktail party. She couldn't imagine why the men were so intent on carrying out their original plans. How dangerous was that? And foolish.

Of course Janie had told them so. Repeatedly. And had been ignored except for a few raised eyebrows and a promise of increased guards and patrols.

"How do you think diplomats and people in political office handle getting together?" Brad asked her. "I'll tell you how. They beef up security and forge ahead. If they hid every time somebody had it in for them, we'd never see them out in public."

She shrugged. "I suppose you're right. They didn't find any clue to the last shooter?"

"An ejected shell casing. There were no prints on it and the manufacturer is common."

"Terrific."

"Well, you did ask."

"You don't have to sound so nonchalant. Somebody tried to kill you."

"Or you."

Janie tried to suppress a shudder. "Or me. If they even knew who we were. Have you and the chief thought of that? Suppose they were just after anybody who was staying here?"

"It did cross our minds. Chase got home in the dawn hours, too, so we can also include him."

"What does he look like?" Janie asked, wondering if she'd seen him.

"Tall and blond. I doubt anybody would mistake me for him."

"Well, aren't you just a fountain of good news." She made a silly face on purpose. "Now what?"

Judging by the changing expressions flashing across Brad's face, he wasn't all that certain. He did, however, manage to give her a sensible answer. "We're hoping that the party tomorrow evening will bring this all to a head."

"Do you honestly think it's fair for Armbruster or any of you to expose innocent civilians to the kind of threat you and I have been facing?"

"Wes and Harold have explained enough to let individuals choose. It's our hope that those who do attend will include the wealthy drug ring backers we're targeting. They wouldn't be afraid to come since the problems originate with them and their underlings."

Janie shook her head slowly, thoughtfully. "Okay, I'll go along with your plan, up to a point, but I can't imagine any criminals being that brazen. Or that foolish."

"Give any man enough money and he thinks he can't be touched," Brad countered.

"Maybe." Janie started to turn away. "See you later." There were dresses upstairs to try on and she had yet to meet Mrs. Armbruster or Chase. That was something she intended to ask Nancy to help her do ASAP.

And then what? Who knew? One thing was certain. She was going to ask Nancy or one of the burly bodyguards to walk her dog for her, at least until after the party. Hopefully, in about twenty-four hours they'd have the answers Brad and Wes sought.

If not, she mused as she reluctantly accepted the alternative, she was *not* going to be a happy camper.

Brad cornered his police chief in an upper hallway and they ducked into Wes's room for an impromptu discussion.

"So, what's your take on the kid? Chase? You knew him fairly well before, right?"

Sighing, Wes nodded. "Yes. I've watched him grow up. Harold and I didn't socialize a whole lot these past few years but I doubt Chase has changed much. He always acted kind of superior. Not nearly as friendly as his father."

Brad took a deep, settling breath and asked a question he'd held back until now. "Do you think he could have had anything to do with Wesley Jr.'s killing?"

"Who, Chase?" The chief was slowly shaking his head as if pondering the notion. "I strongly doubt it. And remember, he's been out of the country since the funeral."

"Did he go to it? I was watching for outside threats so I have to admit I didn't notice the normal mourners."

Appearing puzzled, Wes said, "Beats me. I hardly recall being there myself. Everything is a blur. A few important instances are locked in my memory but overall I'm a terrible witness."

"That's understandable. There was a guest book, right? Maybe you could ask your ex-wife to check that for us."

"No," Wes said flatly. "I may have her give the box of memorabilia to one of my officers and ask him or her to look, but no way am I asking Annie. We packed everything away immediately and stored it. Going through that stuff would be far too painful for her."

"Sorry." He truly was, and yet he knew that every scrap of information they could glean was critical to assembling a complete picture. Why hadn't he thought of asking for a witness list when the team of detectives was putting it together?

"I'll see it's done. And I'll have them compile a total roster, although I suspect that anybody who was there for nefarious purposes would not have signed in."

"They may have if they were trying to appear innocent," Brad countered. He paused while Wes texted their station and gave the order, then continued by asking, "What about the father? Is there any chance—"

Wes's nostrils flared in anger. "Stop there. Don't say another word. Harold Armbruster is like a brother to me. There's no way he's involved in what happened to my son. Or in what's been happening to you and Miss Kirkpatrick since the hospital incident. Got that?"

Brad almost saluted. "Yes, sir. Again, I'm sorry."

"You should be." Wes dismissed him by opening the door to his room and gesturing. "I'll see you at dinner."

"Right." Clearly he was being dismissed.

That was too bad because he had a couple more questions he wanted answered, one of them being whether or not Armbruster had done thorough background checks on all of his staff, especially the pilots.

Starting down the stairs, Brad wished he'd encounter Janie again. Being separated from her, even when she was in her room getting fitted for a party dress, bothered him. He felt as if he should be with her. Watching. Protecting. Defending her the way he had when they'd heard the rifle shot.

Vivid recall made his gut knot. If it weren't for his promises to his chief and the sworn duty to uphold the law no matter what, he'd pack up Janie and hit the road again. They'd probably be just as safe doing that as they were staying on the estate, particularly because there had been such clear warning signs.

Overcome with concern, Brad paused and closed his eyes for a few moments. *Lord, stay with us and help me decide what to do? Please?*

No bolts from the blue or booming ethereal voices provided his answer. He hadn't expected them to. What he had hoped for was the sense of inner peace he often gained when talking to God.

This time, however, all he got was a shiver up his spine and an increased sense of foreboding.

"Maybe for the best," he murmured, continuing down the stairs. Peace was only beneficial when it was real. Complacency, on the other hand, would—could—get him killed. And Janie, too.

That thought was so unacceptable he pivoted and scaled the staircase once again. Long strides took him to her door. He knocked. "Janie?"

If she did reply, it was drowned out by yipping so rapid and high-pitched it pained his ears.

The door eased open a crack. Nancy peered out. "Yes?"

"Is Janie okay?"

"Sure. Why wouldn't she be?"

Brad sighed audibly. "Right. Good question. Sorry to bother you."

From inside he heard Janie ask, "Is that Brad?"

So he called out, "Yes!"

"Come on in and help me decide which dress to wear."

If Nancy hadn't stepped back, he would have pushed her out of his way. Happily, she gave ground.

Brad's gaze lit on Janie and his breath was stolen by the sight of her in a totally different role. "Whoa. Awesome, lady."

It pleased him to see her grin. "You like this one?" She tugged at the thin shoulder straps. "It's awfully low-cut."

He had little doubt he would have loved seeing her in any dress Nancy had chosen. "I like red."

"You don't think it makes me look too pale?"

"I don't know. Why don't you try the blue one?" He pointed. "Over there."

"I kind of liked that one, too." She

waved. "Okay. Leave. It'll just take a second to change."

Although Brad did step out, he leaned his back against the closed door. The women's voices reached him and he considered moving farther away, then changed his mind. Listening might be wrong, but if he heard Nancy express something of interest, he could set aside his guilty conscience.

When he heard one of them mention Chase, he leaned closer. It only took a minute or two for him to be glad he had.

With her back to Nancy, Janie asked, "Anything more you can tell me about Chase or his family? I mean, I'm not asking you to divulge all their secrets but I know it would help me hold my own in casual conversations at the party."

"I'm not sure how I can help. Chase is maturing but he still seems like a dumb teenager to me. I guess that's partly because Wesley Jr. was so mature in comparison."

"He was?"

"Yes," Nancy answered. "I've heard Mr. Armbruster refer to him as an *old soul* more than once. He took life seriously. Chase didn't. At least he didn't before Wes died. Maybe losing his best friend has forced him to grow up some."

"I can see where it would," Janie answered.

Brad could tell she was moving around in the room because her voice faded some of the time. Like now. Straining, he heard her say something else about Wesley but the details were too faint to make out.

"What about the Armbrusters?" Janie asked.

"What about them?"

"Well, what's your impression of them?"

"They're rich. What else is there to say?"

"You said the wife didn't come from money. Is she easy to get along with?"

"She will be for you, I imagine." Something else was mumbled. Brad held his breath.

Janie's voice was much closer to the closed door when Brad heard her say, "I thought you told me you didn't date Chase."

As Nancy replied, "I didn't," the door opened. Brad lost his balance and almost fell in.

Facing Janie, he recovered and smiled. "Caught me napping."

"Come on in. What do you think of this one?"

A whirl of soft blue skirt wrapped around her calves as she turned in a circle in front of him. The color matched her eyes and it took his breath away. Not to mention her silky blond hair and bright smile.

He recovered. "I like it."

"I think this is the one," Janie told Nancy. "It not only fits like a dream, having it on makes me feel like Cinderella."

Nancy was the only one in the room not smiling. Brad saw her eye Janie, then say, "Just remember what I told you. If you're looking for your Prince Charming, Chase Armbruster is not him."

"Not a problem," Janie said with a nervous-sounding chuckle.

Because she was no longer making eye contact with him, Brad had to wonder if she was picturing him in that role. Hopefully not. His presence at the party was strictly work related. And, technically, so was hers.

He sobered. There was nothing wrong with letting Janie have a little fun at the same time. Judging by the way she looked in that dress, she was certainly going to attract plenty of attention, and being in a crowd would help safeguard her.

That, and the gun he intended to carry beneath the tuxedo he was about to be fitted for. If it wouldn't hide the gun and holster, he intended to refuse to dress that way, period.

Armbruster's reputation mattered a lot less to Brad than keeping Janie safe did. The way he saw it, his biggest problem was no longer the suspected drug lords who might attend. The real dilemma was how he could do his job while still being the man Janie Kirkpatrick needed.

Thoughts of their time together ran through his mind in a kaleidoscope of color and sound. *And emotion.*

He stepped closer. Took her hand. Pulled her into his arms and pretended to whirl her around the room in a parody of dance.

Ending at the doorway again, he released her and made a theatrical bow before ducking into the hallway. Having her in his arms in such an innocent situation was all he would permit himself. They had to succeed in finding an end to this fiasco. They just had to.

Before it was too late. For everybody.

TWENTY-TWO

Looking sophisticated in the fabulous blue party dress, Janie studied herself in the full-length mirror. Meg Armbruster had been as lovely to her as Nancy had predicted, insisting on loaning her some blue sapphire jewelry to match her chosen outfit. The necklace was a delicate pendant, and the earrings were chandelier drops that swung when she moved.

Janie had protested having her hair swept up by a professional stylist and makeup done by the woman Meg had hired to do her own, yet she had to admit that the effect was stunning.

Clearly, the older woman had been pleased, too. "Oh, my, yes. I was right.

Putting up your lovely long hair is perfect with that dress and earrings."

"If it stays there," Janie quipped, slightly embarrassed to be out of her comfort zone. "If not, I'll pull it back into a ponytail the way I wear it at work."

Meg laughed gaily. "Oh, honey, just relax and enjoy the party. Nothing is going to fall apart."

If you only knew, Janie thought. Harold knew what was going on in his home but did his wife? And what about Chase? If he was as undisciplined as Nancy had hinted, was he liable to mess up their plans just by being himself?

The most important question she had was, how in the world were Brad and his chief going to pinpoint a drug lord from among a roomful of partyers? That was the real flaw in their plan, and unless they knew something they hadn't shared with her, she didn't have much hope of success.

Pulling Janie away from her musings, Meg took her arm at the elbow and escorted her to the top of the stairs. There, she paused and patted her hand. "Ready?"

Janie giggled. "No. But I'm going, anyway."

"Brave girl." Meg, too, was laughing softly. "Just remember what I've told you. You are no less a person than anybody you'll meet tonight."

"And not any better, either," Janie added. "I don't think I had that problem until you loaned me all this jewelry. Thank you so much for everything."

"My pleasure." She released her hold on Janie's arm and gestured. "After you."

One hand resting on the banister, Janie started down the stairs. At that moment she was less worried about criminals than she was about falling in the heels Meg had found for her. Yes, she felt amazing, but no, she wasn't a bit relaxed.

The ground floor seemed a lot more user-friendly in the heels so Janie stepped aside to wait for her hostess. Meg was the picture of elegance in a sweeping silver gown and diamonds. Knowing the older woman had not grown up in this kind of home, Janie admired her even more for her casual grace and aplomb. If anyone fit in here, it was Mrs. Armbruster.

Once again, Meg paused next to Janie and announced to those nearby, "I'd like you all to meet the daughter of a college friend of mine who has come to stay with us for a bit. This is Alice."

Shocked to have been renamed, Janie forced an amiable smile. She'd do well to remember who she was supposed to be for the evening. Relating it to a child's story, she was able to cement the new name in her memory. This might not be Wonderland to everybody else but it sure was to her. Wow. Champagne glasses and silver trays of tiny bites of food were being offered by servers in black-and-white uniforms. A string quartet played softly in the background. Flower arrangements perfumed the foyer, dining room and living room.

A whiff of fresh, cool air reached Janie's shoulders and drew her eyes to the French doors. As she'd expected, they were half-open. And well guarded.

Strangers kept greeting her. She answered, smiled and nodded politely. But her mind was not on her manners. It was centered on one of the men she saw standing guard at the open door. He looked familiar somehow. Yet there was something about him that gave her the shivers and had nothing to do with night air.

I need to find Brad, she told herself. Moving farther from the questionable guard, she began to wend her way toward the only place she'd felt totally at ease: the kitchen.

Revelers pressed in on her, making it hard to navigate on the stilettos. She wobbled several times and was righted by others who intimated that she might be drunk. Janie smiled and let the error stand, deciding it was better to be thought intoxicated than to be seen as an interloper.

She sought temporary refuge next to a large flower arrangement and peeked out. The guard she'd noticed was looking straight at her, as if he'd recognized her, too.

As she straight-armed into the kitchen, she almost toppled a server bearing a tray.

"So sorry. Have you seen...?" Words failed her. Brad was standing by the table with Wes. His hair had been cut and he was completely clean-shaven. If she had not been looking expressly for him, she might have passed by without notice.

No, she corrected. She would have noticed. Every woman there was bound to. When he looked up, recognized her and smiled, she almost tottered off her heels again.

Beside her in the blink of an eye, Brad took her arm. "Are you all right?"

"Yes. No." She leaned his way to speak aside. "There's somebody out there I think I recognize."

Brad increased the hold on her arm. "Leave it to the private citizen to be the first to spot a clue." He looked to Wes. "I'm going to take Janie back out to the party so she can try to ID some guy. We'll come back as soon as we confirm."

"I'm coming with you," Wes insisted. "I haven't gone through all this to stand down when we finally have a lead."

Janie would have preferred to show Brad first and get his opinion rather than get the chief's hopes up but this was out of her hands. Then again, it occurred to her as they reentered the gala that she was better off with two armed men at her side than with only one.

When they neared the French doors, however, she noted that they were now closed. No one was standing guard.

Her heart leaped, then bottomed out. "They're gone. He's gone. The one I thought looked familiar isn't there anymore."

Brad slipped his arm around Janie's waist the way he had when he was pretending to dance upstairs and led her to a spot in front of the string quartet where a few couples were attempting to find room to follow the music.

The scent of roses filled his senses as he bent to whisper in her ear. "We'll hang out here for now. As I turn you, check out what you see in the distance. If one of our old enemies is here, chances are others are."

"That's not very comforting."

"I've got you," he replied, drawing her as close as he dared and holding tight to her hand. The way she returned his unspoken affection as she touched his shoulder was so meaningful he shivered.

The job, Brad kept repeating to himself. *Stay alert. Do the job.*

He did exactly that, also searching the faces in the crowd, including the waitstaff and burly guards.

Although there was no way to discount the rifle shot, they hadn't actually seen any concrete signs of their enemies until this evening, meaning whoever Janie had noticed had likely come with one of the guests, as he and Wes had hoped. Unless they spotted another recognizable face they were going to have to keep looking for that particular man, then find out who he worked for in order to steer their investigation in the right direction. Yes, Wes's plan was flawed. But no, he wasn't about to refuse to carry it out.

He felt Janie jerk in his arms, then tense every muscle. "Where?" is all Brad asked.

"At the bottom of the stairs," she whispered.

Brad turned her. Checked that area himself. The only person he saw who stood out was Chase Armbruster. Could the youth have been back in the States before his father knew it and be behind some of the attacks?

"That's Chase. Are you sure?"

Urging him to circle again, Janie leaned to one side while Brad kept her on an even keel. When she looked back up at him her eyes were wide, glistening. "No. Not the kid. The guy he's talking to. He's half-hidden behind the fern."

Brad tried again. This time, he saw not

only the burly thug who had accosted Janie in the hospital parking lot, he recognized another man. Unless his imagination was taking over, that one had shot at him after crashing into his first truck.

He realized how tightly he was embracing Janie when she protested with a firm shove. "I need to breathe."

"Sorry." Brad tried to see more. There were several others in the group Chase was with. If they'd turn slightly, he knew he could probably tell enough. The question now was, did he and Wes want to isolate Chase to question him? They were guests of the young man's father, yet it seemed best to move in immediately.

Spotting Wes from across the room, Brad caught the chief's eye and leaned his head toward Chase in a silent signal.

Wes nodded back at him. Brad stopped pretending to dance and eased Janie to the sidelines, his hand at the small of her back.

"We'll go talk to the kid. You stay here

by Meg and mingle if she does. Just don't go off on your own."

He almost smiled at the eye roll Janie gave him before she commented, "Well, duh."

"I know, honey. You're resourceful and brave. And that's worked for you so far. But tonight is altogether different. You can't afford to be isolated and I can't take you with me to question Chase."

"Why not?"

Brad wouldn't have been too surprised if she'd stamped her foot like an unhappy child but she stood firm. "Because it's a guy thing, okay? He's a lot more likely to talk if there are no strangers there."

"You don't know him that well, do you?"

"No, but Wes will take the lead. It should be his privilege, anyway, given the history he has with the family. Remember, his son was Chase's best friend."

Capitulation was plain on Janie's face. Brad stepped back, making sure she was steady despite the tension. "Meg is over there, by the viola player. See? Get going. I'll keep an eye on you."

Janie pouted. "Oh, for crying out loud, just go. Do your job before the bad guys get away again."

Wishing he had more than one sworn officer for backup, Brad stood tall and started across the room, converging on Chase Armbruster at the same time the chief did. Yes, they had been assured of extra security people by their host. And yes, he'd met new bodyguards before leaving an earlier planning session. Nevertheless, it was getting harder and harder to tell friends from foes and Brad didn't like feeling out of control. Not one little bit.

He edged up to Chase's shoulder to block an escape as Wes greeted him forcefully head-on. "There you are, son. Good to see you again. How was your stay in the tropics?" He clapped the youth's shoulder. "Great tan, by the way."

Instead of the wary greeting Brad had expected, Chase wrapped Wes in a bear hug and began to weep.

Whether the emotional upheaval was due to shared sorrow or plain guilt wasn't apparent. It did, however, bode well for their upcoming grilling. A young man who was so overcome by merely seeing the father of his lost friend again would be far more likely to open up during questioning.

Wes put a fatherly arm around Chase's shoulders and urged him toward the front door, clearly intending to seek privacy outside.

As Brad prepared to follow he casually scanned the area where he'd left Janie. Meg was still holding a champagne flute and laughing with guests.

And Janie? Brad bobbed his head back and forth, peering through the crowd. In that stunning dress Janie had stood out like a beacon of blue sky peeking through a summer storm.

"Wes!" He lunged for the chief's arm and stopped him. "I don't see her."

Chase looked surprised while Wes's expression reflected Brad's fears.

"Go!" the chief ordered. "Find her."

* * *

Janie had done everything right. Except for one little thing, she realized belatedly. She'd let herself be crowded too near to one of the exits.

An aura of menace tickled her senses an instant before someone grabbed her around the waist and lifted her off the ground. She would have screamed if he hadn't also clamped a hand over her mouth and nose. Grasping the abductor's forearm with both hands she tried to use her body weight to pitch him over her head but she'd acted too late. He already had too much advantage.

Gasping for air she felt her head starting to throb. Surroundings were spinning. Fading. *No. Wait.* That was darkness. Cool air. They were outside and moving fast away from the mansion, she knew, because her body was bouncing in time with her captor's long strides.

In a crowd that size had no one seen them take her? It seemed impossible and yet she didn't hear any shouting or feel her kidnapper falter.

Air! Janie's brain was screaming silently. She had to have air. Able to part her lips a little she managed to grab a quick mouthful of oxygen before the man moved his hand. That was all she needed. She bit the fleshy part of his palm.

Jerking away he howled. Janie didn't care how much she'd hurt him. All she cared about was being able to breathe again.

Shooting pain in her side when she did that cleared her head, leaving her with the suspicion the thug might have broken her ribs during the abduction. If not, they were definitely bruised. All she hoped at the moment was that no fractures would be displaced and do internal damage.

Someone else took control. He and her original attacker dragged her into one of the aircraft hangars at the bottom of the hill while she screamed as loud as she could.

"No! Let me go. Help!"

Lights inside the hangar seemed blindingly bright. Janie blinked, seeing a small group of people waiting. Someone gave her arm a sharp pull before commanding, "Quiet. Or else."

"Or else what?" Not only was her vision adjusting, Janie was getting mad. Really mad, which wasn't the smartest reaction, she realized. It was also almost impossible to subdue.

"Or else we make you." The barrel of a gun was pressed to her temple.

She sagged against the firm holds on her upper arms, letting her captors help support her while she did what she should have done in the first place. Pray.

In this instance, however, she kept her eyes wide open. Only two of the men present were familiar. They stepped aside and let someone through to the front to confront her.

Janie gasped and said the first thing that popped into her mind. "Did they kidnap you, too?"

Nancy laughed. "Not quite."

"Then what…?"

More laughter echoed off the metal walls of the hangar. "Ah, I see you're starting to see the whole picture."

"No. No, I'm not. You were so sweet to me. How can you be involved in all this?"

Nancy shrugged, shaking her head slowly and smiling. "Long story. Let's just say I fell for the wrong guy at the wrong time."

"Who? You're, what, twenty, twenty-five?"

"Maybe I don't like men my own age," Nancy taunted.

The first one who came to mind was Harold Armbruster, but try as she might, Janie couldn't imagine Nancy falling for him.

A hint of disgust must have shown on her face because Nancy laughed wryly again. "No, not the old man. The handsome, young one."

"But how does that figure into all of this? Why kill Wesley Jr.? What was he to you?"

"Nothing. Just a bothersome bug crawling on the wall. But his cop father was going to be a problem."

"What made you think so?" Janie realized she might be the only one to ever hear this confession but she had to know the answers to these questions.

"Because he told me," Nancy said flatly. "The idiot told me he was going to ask his father to bail out him and Chase. Just like that. They'd gotten involved in drug smuggling and thought they could walk away scot-free, with no consequences."

"I'm confused. What part did you play?"

"Are you kidding? I'd set up Chase to marry me. All that money. Plus, he was kind of cute if you like them immature."

Unbelievable. "So, let me get this straight," Janie said, "you were convinced that getting rid of Wesley would fix things for you and Chase? What did he have to say about it?"

"That wimp? I never told him until it was over. When I did, he skipped out and left me here to wait and wait. Until you showed up, I wondered how long it was going to take him to come home."

"His parents didn't suspect you? I mean, they must have known you and Chase were having a fling."

Nancy erupted angrily. "A fling? Is that what you think it was? He loved me. *Loves* me. Just wait. You'll see. As soon as you and your boyfriend and his cop boss back off, everything will be back to normal and I'll have my way."

"Don't you see?" Janie argued. "It won't be that easy. Harold and Meg are bound to figure things out eventually."

That brought such raucous laughter from the young woman Janie was taken aback. As soon as the noise died down she asked, "Why is that so funny?"

Nancy was shaking her head and looking to the assembled thugs. "I told you they didn't have a clue. See?"

There was only one conclusion Janie could reach without more concrete information. She straightened and stood tall, facing what she now felt was her ultimate fate. "The drug lord we've been looking for is Harold Armbruster, isn't it?"

"You win first prize."

"So, now you're going to kill me?" The words Janie spoke seemed as if they were coming from a stranger, as if she were standing apart and watching a scary movie.

"Not quite yet," Nancy said. She motioned with the gun barrel. "Put her over there until we get them all. We may need her later."

Stumbling, Janie was bound with rough cord and shoved down into a corner next to a drum of oil or gas. Fumes definitely tagged it as a petroleum product. She'd lost one of her shoes in the process so she slipped off the remaining one and slid it behind her as she sat on the floor. The spike heel wasn't a particularly efficient weapon but it beat trying to fight back with her wrists tied together.

She watched one of the men pull out a cell phone and dial. When he said, "We have her, sir. Send the others," Janie's heart fell.

The trap was set for Brad and Wes, and she was the bait.

TWENTY-THREE

Brad had scoured the familiar areas around the estate to no avail, so he returned to Wes. "Can't find her. We need to search the whole house."

"In a minute," Wes managed. "Chase may be able to tell us where she is." Beside him, the blond youth was in tears, gasping out details of his unwilling part in his best friend's murder. The chief was silently shedding tears, too.

Brad interrupted, "How did you get so deep in the first place? I can understand why you and Wesley Jr. were pulled into the drug scene. You didn't watch who you associated with. But what brought you so far that you killed him?"

"Not—not me," Chase stammered. "I

didn't know. I swear I didn't. Not till it was already too late."

"Then why leave the country if you were innocent?"

Face flushed, eyes red and puffy, Chase cast a glance at the mansion behind them. "Because I couldn't stay here. Not anymore. Not knowing…"

"What?" Brad demanded. "What did you know that you're not saying?"

That brought soul-racking sobs instead of a verbal answer. If Chase was trying to tell them what Brad suspected he was, this part of the case was going to be almost as rough on the police chief as anything so far, with the exception of losing his only son.

"It's your father, isn't it?" Brad asked. He saw Wes start to object, then stop, stunned.

Chase was nodding. "That's why he invited you here. At least I think it is. Nancy was brought in on it, too, after Dad learned there was going to be a woman with you."

"Janie? You targeted Janie?" Brad felt as if he'd burst from overwhelming sorrow.

"Not me!" Chase grabbed Brad's forearm through the sleeve of his tuxedo jacket. "Please believe me. I'm not behind all this."

Brad shook him off and grabbed both his shoulders. An adult's muscles trembled beneath his hands while a child's heart shed tears of remorse. "All right. What else? Do you know how we were supposed to be targeted?"

Chase nodded, speechless, until Brad gave him a hard shake. "How? Talk!"

"I—I'm not sure. Nancy was supposed to get her to leave the party, I think."

"And then what? Where were they taking her?"

"I don't know. Dad figured out I wasn't going to help him so he kept me in the dark. I was trying to find out more from his guards when you pulled me away."

"Can Janie be in the house?" Wes asked. All he got was a shrug.

"I've searched the yard," Brad told him.

"There's no way one man can cover this whole estate by himself."

"You're right. I'll call the state police for backup. In the meantime, I'll take the house and start by searching her room. Which one is it?"

"I'll show you. Follow me!"

He pushed startled people out of his way. The stairs flew by beneath his feet. The hallway was a blur. Brad burst into the room where his beloved Janie had been staying. It was empty except for her little dog.

In all the excitement he'd forgotten about Pixie. Instead of attacking and sinking those needlelike teeth into his ankle again, she took one look at him and ran to the window, paws on the sill, whining at the darkness outside.

Brad joined her. Slid open the lower section. Tried to listen despite her yips. "Is that where she is, girl? Do you know for sure?"

The little dog wiggled all over and jumped at him. Brad scooped her up, turning to Wes. "Keep searching the house. I'm going back out. *We're* going back out."

"She's not a tracking dog. She's hardly a dog at all," Wes said with undisguised disgust. "Don't kid yourself."

"I prayed for help. Maybe this is it. I'm not about to discount any leads I get."

His chief waved him off. "Fine. Go. As soon as I've completed a quick sweep of the upstairs I'm going to pin down my good buddy, Harold." Wes patted the holster beneath his jacket. "He and I are about to have a chat."

"But please, do all you can to find Janie," Brad pleaded. "I can't explain how much she means to me."

"Figured as much." Wes seemed to soften. "Go on, then. You have my prayers, too. Find her."

"I'll do my best."

Leaving his only sure human ally, Brad carried his canine one down the stairs, across the living room and out the French door nearest his last glimpse of Janie.

Several women attending the gala

grinned and reached out to pet Pixie as they passed. Brad skillfully avoided them. He didn't release the dog until they were outside, away from the revelry. Then he placed the little white dog on the grass, prepared to wait and see what she did.

In milliseconds he was sorry he'd neglected a leash. Yipping, short legs churning up grass, Pixie took off as if electrified. Brad was able to keep her in sight only because she was stark white against the dark background.

He began to follow at a dead run. The dog's target was clearly one of the hangars by the private airstrip. He could tell that neither of them was going to slow down until they got there.

Brad watched Pixie disappear into the light emanating from an open hangar door.

He heard the echo of a gunshot. Drew his pistol. And, for the first time in his life, prayed for a dog.

Janie wasn't the only occupant of the hangar to hear Pixie coming. She saw

Nancy aim for the doorway. Heart and mind screaming, her voice shouted, "No!"

She pivoted to search for the discarded shoe, fumbled it for an instant, then held it overhead and threw. It wasn't enough to cause damage but it did make Nancy flinch. The shot went wild. Pixie charged in and made straight for her bound companion.

Janie had never been so glad—or so sad—to see her tiny friend. Nancy must have abandoned poor Pixie when she'd left the house and here she was, smack-dab in the middle of a terrible situation neither of them were likely to survive.

Miracles were for Biblical times, people said, so Janie chose to call her pleas for rescue mere intervention. She didn't really care about semantics as long as somebody came to save her. To save them.

Holding Pixie close she let her little pet lick tears from her cheeks and cuddle close. She'd relied on the dog for comfort before and needed her even more right now.

That isn't all I need, Janie admitted without regret. *I need Brad.*

But not all by himself, she added. Not against all these evil guys and the traitorous young woman. Not even if Wes happened to be with him. There was no way two men could match the firepower already braced to shoot them on sight.

Nancy kept her pistol trained on the open door, waiting. Janie could tell that the guards were waiting, as well. What she wasn't sensing was a unity of purpose among them. A few had fallen back as if unwilling to go along with Nancy's stated plans. Others had drawn guns when she'd fired at Pixie and now held them at their sides as if unsure what to do. Assuming Harold had hired them was no guarantee they'd do the bidding of the maid, even if she really was engaged to Chase.

Minutes ticked by so slowly Janie wanted to scream. Instead, she held her dog close and kept quiet. The less attention she drew, the better, she reasoned. And the longer it took for Brad to realize she was missing and come looking for her, the more chance he'd have of getting local law enforcement backup. Whatever he did, she hoped he didn't try storming the place by himself. That would be akin to suicide.

"Please, Lord, take care of him," Janie prayed in a whisper. "Even if he's not in time to rescue me."

Did she mean that? she wondered. Oh, yes. She loved him that much. The only sad element of her confession was that she might never have the chance to tell him.

One of the guards raised his pistol and aimed at the doorway. "I hear something."

Agreeing because Pixie had also alerted, Janie kept silent.

"Well, go see," Nancy ordered.

A brief glance at his cohorts and he was on his way toward the bay door. He stopped at the edge with his shoulder to the metal frame, then whipped around the corner, ready to fire.

Janie held her breath. Nothing happened. No shots, no shouts, no sounds of any kind.

Nancy called out to him, "What do you see?"

There was no reply.

Without waiting for further orders, the rest of the men fanned out. Some approached the open bay door while others headed for the walk-through exit to the side. Hunkering down with her dog, Janie made herself as small a target as possible. If and when the shooting started, she didn't want to be an accidental casualty.

A deep male voice resounded from outside. "Stand down! That's an order."

Harold? How could it be? He was the drug kingpin, so what was he doing calling off his goons? And what about Brad and Wes? Had they already been eliminated?

That thought resounded in Janie's brain, making bile rise in her throat and her stomach clench with a fist of iron.

"Please, Jesus," was all she could think. The prayer wasn't polished or eloquent but she believed her frantic, intense pleas would be heard, regardless. They had to be. They just had to be.

The guards began to look at each other. One by the door peeked out, then signaled with a wave of his arm.

Janie felt as if a flood of peace and calm was washing over her. She looked up. Harold Armbruster and his son stepped into view.

Behind them, using the father's broad body as a shield, was Wes. Then came Brad, accompanied by the copilot who had frightened her. There was a badge hanging around his neck on a cord and he was wearing a vest that read DEA. He was one of the good guys!

Janie was overcome. Tears filled her eyes and began to streak her cheeks. Brad was there. He was alive.

And he had come for her.

Brad spotted her immediately. Not only had Armbruster surrendered, his guards were doing likewise. The only holdout was the young maid, and Chase was about to disarm her, as well.

Signaling the chief, Brad left him and ran to Janie. Her beautiful dress was tangled and torn, her hair mussed, yet she had never looked more beautiful to him.

She held up her bound wrists. Brad freed her, then took her hands and pulled her to her feet while Pixie circled and barked excitedly as if to ask him what had taken him so long.

Without those towering heels Janie was shorter standing next to him. Perfect in his arms. Perfect in his life, if she'd have him. Conventional dating would be the wisest approach, he'd told himself over and over, but seeing her, holding her close, he couldn't stop himself.

A tender, loving kiss came first. Then he asked, "Are you all right?"

She snuggled against him. "I am now."

"You're sure? Because I wouldn't want you to think I'm taking advantage of your fears."

"The only thing I'm scared of is having to leave you now that your case is solved."

"I have the solution for that." Brad could hear a quaver of pent-up emotion in his voice, could sense the new kind of fear he was experiencing. Well, he figured it was better to know than to keep wondering so he blurted it out. "Marry me."

Janie leaned back slightly, lifted her tear-streaked face to his and nodded. "I thought you'd never ask."

EPILOGUE

A special task force had been formed to debrief everyone involved. By combining the confessions of some of the guards as well as those of Harold Armbruster and Nancy, Brad and Janie were able to piece together enough to figure out the key players in the sad drama. It took months to break up the drug ring as well as exonerate Chase but thankfully the case was almost ready to go to trial.

Poor Meg Armbruster had been kept in the dark throughout the entire operation and had taken her son home to work toward mutual healing. To everyone's relief, the young man had not touched drugs since his best friend's murder. At least something good had come out of all this, Janie mused.

Clad in a white wedding dress that Meg had insisted on gifting her, Janie stood in the rear of the small chapel just outside Jefferson City, gazed down the center aisle at her husband-to-be and smiled wistfully. Her heart was so full of love, so committed to this man, she could hardly contain the joy.

Beautiful music surrounded her. If Brad had not insisted they get to know each other better in a normal way, she would have married him that past fall. But he'd been adamant. And now it was time. Finally.

Her pink-clad maid of honor, a nurse from the hospital where she'd worked when Brad had first come into her life, handed Janie her bridal bouquet, then started down the aisle. The young woman carried two things. In one hand was a be-ribboned bunch of roses. In the other arm she bore a sparkling-clean little white dog with matching bows in her hair.

"I love you," Janie mouthed to her waiting groom.

Grinning from ear to ear he returned a simple, "I love you, too."

Janie blinked back tears of joy, reached out and took the arm of Chief Winterhaven, who was standing in for her absent father. As far as she was concerned, her new extended family was almost as perfect as Brad was.

A tear escaped behind her veil. So happy and blessed she was floating on air, she went forward to meet her future.

* * * * *

If you loved this story,
pick up the previous books
in the Emergency Responders series
from bestselling author
Valerie Hansen:

Fatal Threat
Marked for Revenge

Available now from
Love Inspired Suspense!

Find more great reads at
www.LoveInspired.com

Dear Reader,

By the time you read this, we will all be changed, hopefully for the better. The threat of danger may be new to many of us but it's a daily challenge to emergency responders, especially in the health and law enforcement professions. They may not always acknowledge this sense of jeopardy or be able to name it the way my characters in this story can, but it lurks in the background just the same. Those like Janie and Brad who choose to stand firm and battle evil are to be thanked and praised, and above all supported with our cooperation and prayers.

The search for peace is universal. Reach out to God, trust Jesus and it will be yours.

I love hearing from readers. You can email me at Val@ValerieHansen.com, check out my website at ValerieHansen.com, or find me on Facebook or Instagram.

Blessings,
Valerie Hansen